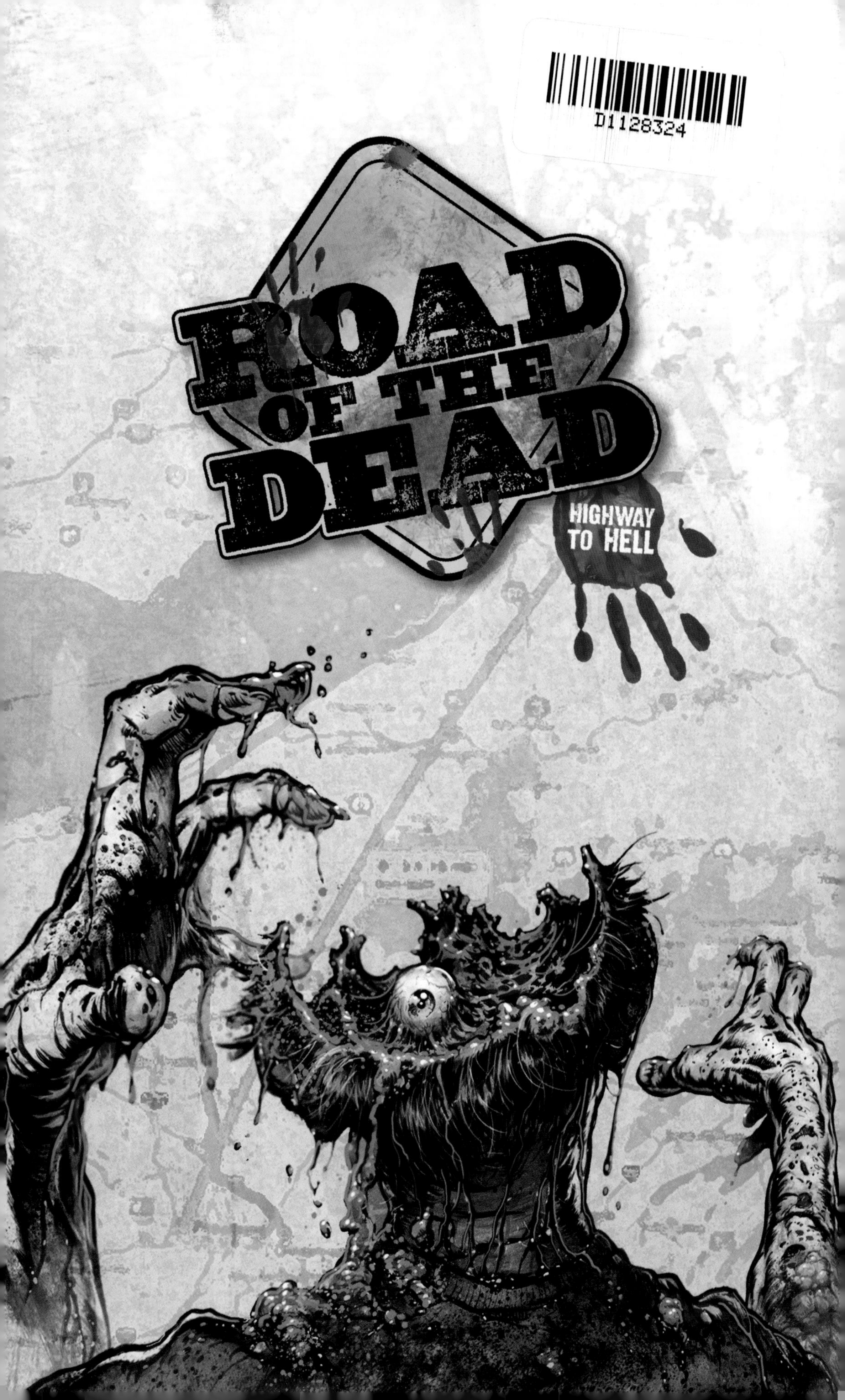
D1128324
ROAD OF THE DEAD
HIGHWAY TO HELL

Become our fan on Facebook **facebook.com/idwpublishing**
Follow us on Twitter **@idwpublishing**
Subscribe to us on YouTube **youtube.com/idwpublishing**
See what's new on Tumblr **tumblr.idwpublishing.com**
Check us out on Instagram **instagram.com/idwpublishing**

COVER ARTIST
SANTÍPEREZ

COVER COLORIST
JAY FOTOS

COLLECTION EDITORS
JUSTIN EISINGER
AND **ALONZO SIMON**

COLLECTION DESIGNER
CLAUDIA CHONG

ISBN: 978-1-68405-478-7 22 21 20 19 1 2 3 4

ROAD OF THE DEAD: HIGHWAY TO HELL. JUNE 2019. FIRST PRINTING.

Originally published as ROAD OF THE DEAD: HIGHWAY TO HELL issues #1–3.

For international rights, contact licensing@idwpublishing.com

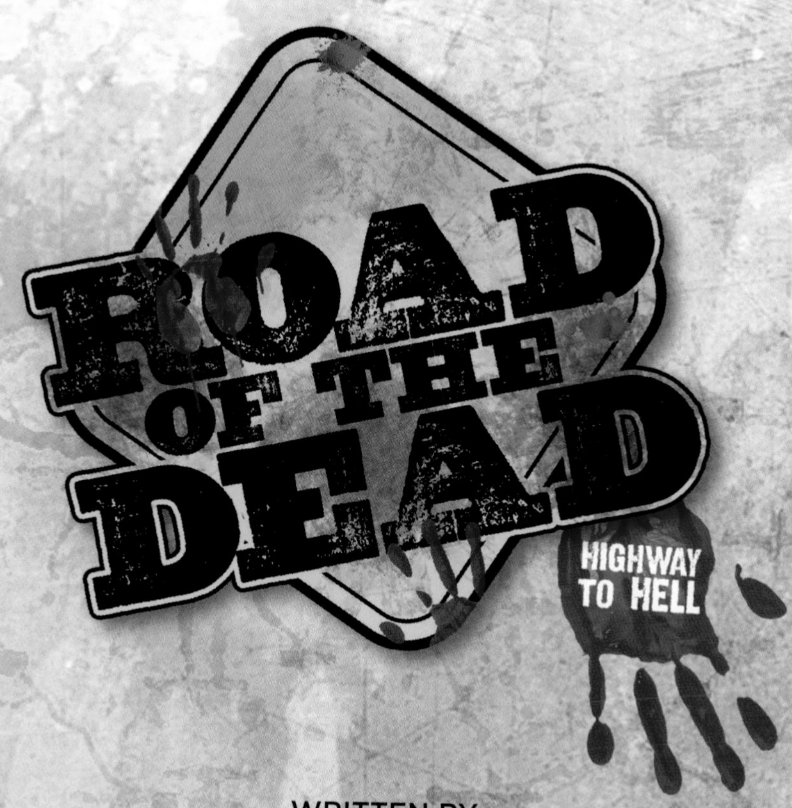

WRITTEN BY
JONATHAN MABERRY

ART BY
DREW MOSS

COLORS BY
JAY FOTOS

LETTERS BY
ROBBIE ROBBINS

SERIES EDITS BY
DAVID HEDGECOCK

ART BY
DREW MOSS
COLORS BY
JAY FOTOS

MY NAME'S STEVE HANSON, U.S. ARMY. I'M A NINETEEN KILO, AN ARMOR CREWMAN IN AN M1 ABRAMS.
JUST RETURNED FROM AFGHANISTAN. SUPPOSED TO ROTATE OUT AND GO THE HELL HOME.
THEN THE DEAD ROSE AND EVERYTHING WENT TO SHIT.
ONE CLUSTERFUCK LATER AND MY TANK CREW'S RUNNING WITH THE 56TH STRYKER BRIGADE COMBAT TEAM, 28TH INFANTRY DIVISION.
EXCEPT THEY DON'T HAVE ANY DAMN STRYKERS LEFT, AND WE'VE BEEN RUNNING FROM ONE CUSTER'S LAST STAND TO THE NEXT. FIGHTING ZOMMED-OUT CIVILIANS WITH A TANK.
A GUY CAN'T EVEN PINCH A LOAF WITHOUT THINGS GOING FROM BAD TO WORSE.
POK POK
POK POK
CHRIST! THERE'S A SWARM OF THE FUCKERS.
POK
POK POK POK POK
OH, JESUS—THEY'RE EVERYWHERE!
SHIT-SHIT-SHIT!
POK POK POK
SON-OF-A...
TOK
HANSON, GET YOUR ASS UP HERE. WE NEED—
AIIIIIEEEE!

GUYS? BURT? TOMMY? LOOT?
WHAT HAPPENED? EVERYONE...
...OKAY?

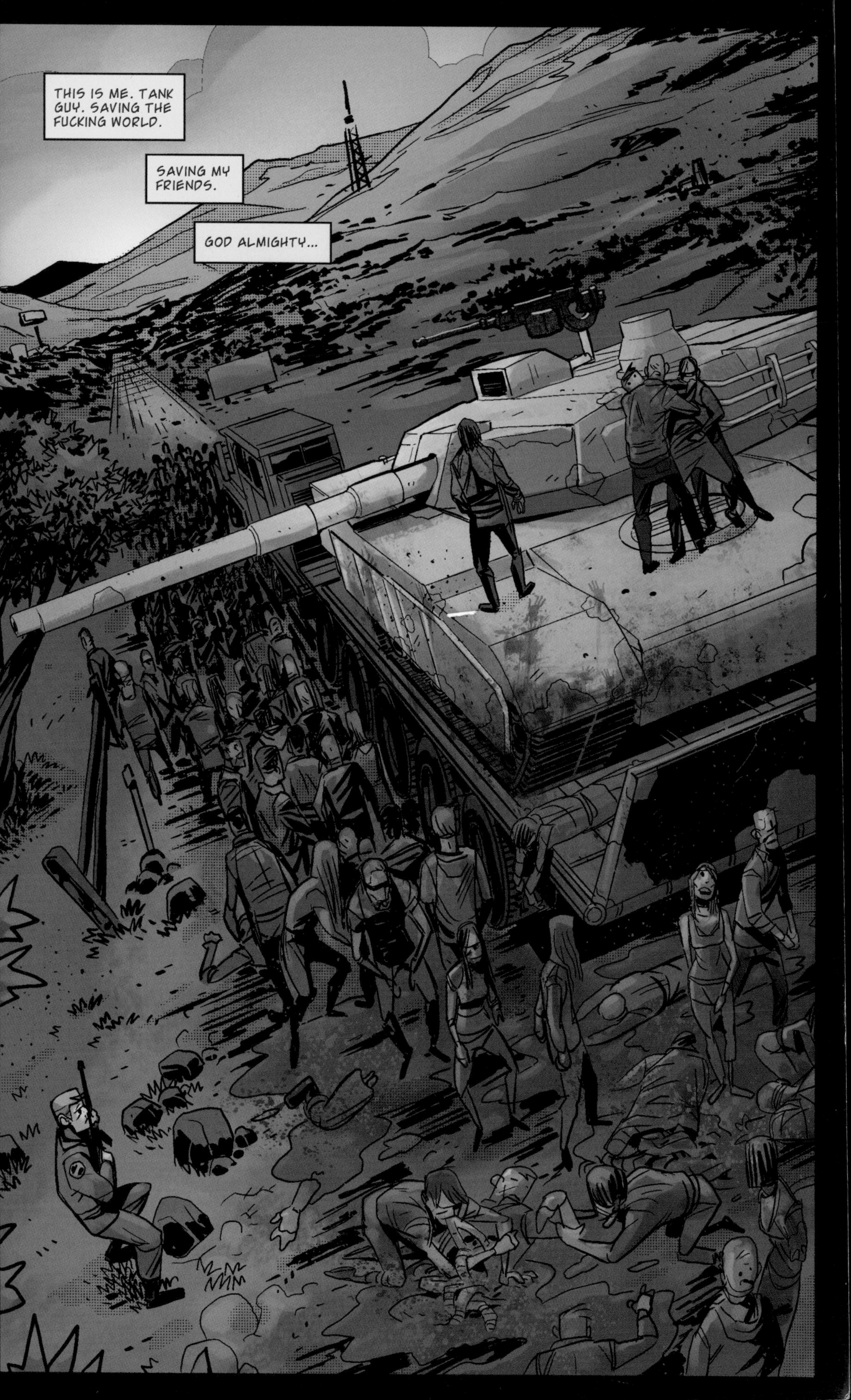
THIS IS ME. TANK GUY. SAVING THE FUCKING WORLD.
SAVING MY FRIENDS.
GOD ALMIGHTY...

JESUS FUCKING CHRIST...
SHIT! SHIT! SHIT! SHIT!
SHIT.
TOMMY? BURT?!
I THINK THIS IS WHY WE'RE LOSING THIS WAR. WE'RE NOT FIGHTING TERRORISTS.
OH GOD. I'M SO SORRY...

WE'RE FIGHTING US.
BLAM
SPLUT
EVERY TIME YOU PULL A TRIGGER, YOU BLOW ANOTHER HOLE IN YOUR OWN HEART.
AHHHHHHHHHHHHHHHHHHHHHHHHHHHHHHH!
HOW THE FUCK CAN ANYONE HOPE TO WIN A WAR LIKE THIS?
HOW? GO ON, TELL ME. HOW?

THIS WAR IS GOING TO MAKE MONSTERS OF US ALL.

OR MAYBE IT ALREADY HAS.

EVERYONE I GIVE A COLD SHIT ABOUT IS DEAD.
MY FAMILY IN PITTSBURGH. MY TANK CREW. EVERYONE ON MY FACEBOOK PAGE. DEAD.

AND I GET TO LIVE BECAUSE I WAS TAKING A SHIT?

IT'S NOT FAIR. THE WORLD IS TOTALLY BUGFUCK NUTS.

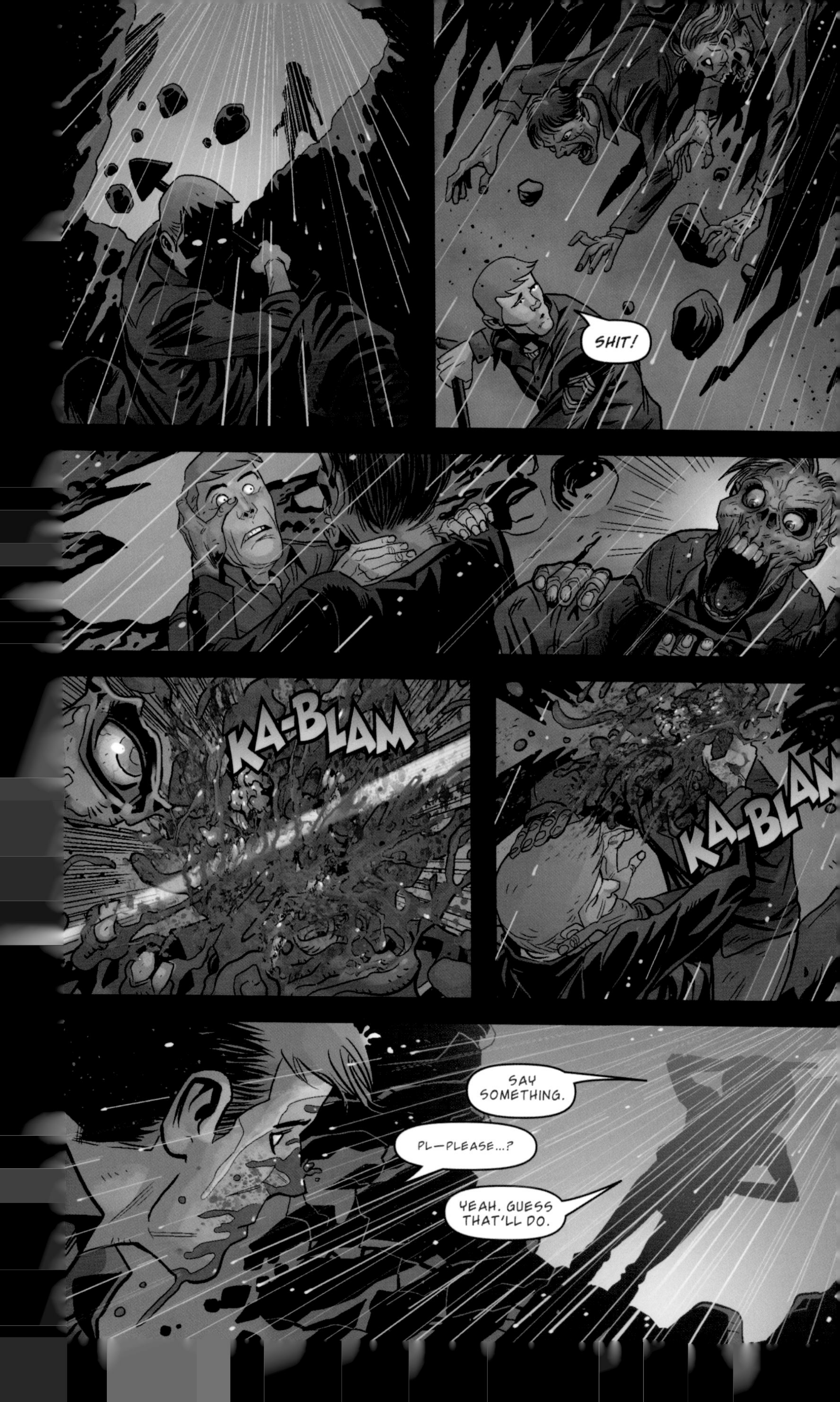
SHIT!
KA-BLAM
KA-BLAM
SAY SOMETHING.
PL—PLEASE...?
YEAH. GUESS THAT'LL DO.

LET'S GET YOU THE FUCK OUT OF THERE ...UNLESS YOU WERE JUST DIGGING YOUR OWN GRAVE.
GOD, NO.
MY NAME'S SHAWN. ASSUME I AM A BADASS. ALSO ASSUME I'M NOT A DICKHEAD. HOW CAN YOU TELL? YOU'RE NOT DEAD IS HOW.
I CAN WORK WITH THAT.
LONG STORY SHORT, I RAN INTO A BUNCH OF IMPORTANT PEOPLE WHO NEED TO GET THE FUCK OUT OF HERE. I'M HELPING THEM GET TO A PLACE IN CANADA.
IMPORTANT... HOW?
IMPORTANT LIKE MAYBE SAVING THE WORLD.
I'M DR. HARRIET JAYNE. MICROBIOLOGIST AND EPIDEMIOLOGIST. I'M ON LOAN FROM THE CDC TO DARPA. MY TEAM HAS BEEN WORKING ON SOMETHING THAT MIGHT REVERSE THE EFFECTS OF THIS PLAGUE.
MY BOSS, GENERAL COPPERHEAD, HAS A SECURE FACILITY SET UP ON WOLFE ISLAND IN THE ST. LAWRENCE RIVER IN ONTARIO. IT HAS A FULL LAB.
WE'RE RIGHT ON THE VERGE OF A BREAKTHROUGH. RESTORING COGNITIVE FUNCTION TO THE REANIMATES. WE THINK WE CAN AWAKEN THEIR MINDS ENOUGH TO INTERRUPT THE AGGRESSION THAT SEEMS TO BE THE CENTRAL COMPONENT OF THIS INFECTION.
WE CAN STOP THEM FROM WANTING TO KILL US. AND EAT US.
GOD ALMIGHTY.

WE WERE ON OUR WAY TO MCKEESPORT. BUNCH OF LOOTERS—BIKERS, ROGUE TRUCKERS, WHATEVER—BEEN STEALING SUPPLIES FROM RESCUE CENTERS.
YOU WERE GOING TO SPANK LOOTERS WITH A FREAKING ABRAMS TANK?
GUESS THE BRASS WANTED TO MAKE A POINT. BUT... WOLFE ISLAND SOUNDS LIKE A BETTER PLAY.
DAMN STRAIGHT. BUT CAN YOU DRIVE THIS BIG MOTHERHUMPER?
THAT'S MY JOB. I CAN DRIVE ANYTHING.
YEAH, BUT DOES THAT MEAN YOU KNOW HOW TO *FIGHT* IN THIS THING?
FUCK YEAH. DID THREE TOURS IN THE BIG SANDBOX.
ANY—GODDAMN—THING GETS IN OUR WAY, AND I'LL BLOW THEM BACK TO JESUS.
WITH THE PEDAL ALL THE WAY DOWN, SHE'LL DO FORTY-FIVE MILES ON A PAVED ROAD. TWENTY-FIVE OVER DIRT.
BUT SHE'S A PIG, SHAWN. EVEN WITH A 500-GALLON TANK, SHE'LL ONLY GO 250 MILES.
IT'S ALMOST TWICE THAT TO WOLFE LAKE. MORE IF WE HAVE TO DETOUR.
SO, SHE'S FAT, SLOW, AND SHE DRINKS TOO MUCH. SOUNDS LIKE MY SECOND WIFE.
THAT'S WHY WE USUALLY HAUL HER AROUND ON THAT M1070 FLATBED OVER THERE. IT MOUNTS A 2000-GALLON REFILL TANK, TOO.

BETTER HAUL ASS, MAN. WE'RE ABOUT TO HAVE A REAL PARTY HERE.
MOVING AS FAST I CAN. THIS OLD GIRL WEIGHS 60 TONS.
THEN IT'D MAKE A RIGHT FINE HEADSTONE FOR WHAT'S LEFT OF YOU, 'CAUSE WE GOT HALF THE POPULATION OF PITTSBURGH COMING FOR LUNCH. GUESS WHAT'S ON THE MENU?
MONROEVILLE MALL
WE HAVE EVERYTHING YOU NEED!
KA-BLAM

YEAH. WE FOUND THE SCIENCE NERDS.
DADDY'S GONNA ROCK...
BUT... DUDE, 'MEMBER YOU SAID WE NEEDED SOME EXTRA OOMPH IF WE WANTED TO SELL THOSE CDC FUCKERS TO THE HIGHEST BIDDER?
DADDY'S GONNA ROLL...
WELL, BETTER GRAB YOUR NUTSACK WITH BOTH HANDS, 'CAUSE YOU AIN'T GONNA BELIEVE WHAT I'M LOOKING AT RIGHT NOW.

WOLFE LAKE 514 MILES
MAYBE I'M CRAZY, BUT THIS IS KIND OF FUN.
'MAYBE'...?
JESUS CHRIST, MAN. SOME OF THOSE THINGS WERE MY FRIENDS.
KEEP THINKING THAT WAY AND YOU'LL LOSE YOUR SHIT BEFORE WE GET HALFWAY THERE.
SO... WHAT? I'M SUPPOSED TO JUST TURN OFF MY COMPASSION? I KNEW THOSE GUYS. BEEN WITH SOME OF THEM FOR YEARS.
I WAS WITH MY BROTHER FOR LONGER THAN THAT, BUT WHEN PUSH CAME TO SHOVE, I BLEW HIS HEAD OFF.
MY WIFE, TOO. MY AUNT.
MY BABY GIRL.
I KILLED 'EM ALL. AND HALF THE PEOPLE ON MY BLOCK. KIDS I GREW UP WITH. KNOWN SINCE KINDERGARTEN. SHOT ALL THOSE MOTHERFUCKERS.
THE WORLD AIN'T THE WORLD NO MORE.
IT'S CHANGED. SO WE HAVE TO CHANGE, TOO.

GET.
THE.
FUCK.
OFF!
THE DEAD WANTED US.
THEY WANTED US SO BAD.
WE HAD TO EARN IT. EVERY INCH. EVERY YARD. EVERY MILE.
NOT SURE IF SHAWN HAD ALREADY LOST HIS SHIT.
OR IF HE WAS WHERE WE ALL NEEDED TO BE.
I DON'T KNOW.
ALL I KNEW FOR SURE WAS THE SCARED YOUNG WOMAN SITTING BESIDE ME THOUGHT SHE COULD FIX THIS.
AND MAYBE 'CRAZY' WAS THE ONLY WAY TO GET HER TO SAFETY. IF SO, WHO WOULD WE ALL BE WHEN THIS WAR WAS WON?

WE GOT CLEAR OF THE WOODS. LEFT THE MALL BEHIND. STARTED BURNING OFF THE MILES.
YOU REALLY THINK YOU CAN BEAT THIS THING, DR. JAYNE?
IT'S HARRIET... AND, YES. I THINK WE HAVE A REAL CHANCE.
I HAVE A TON OF RESEARCH ON THIS FLASH DRIVE.
A REAL
SHE SAID.
THERE'S A MILLION THEORIES ON HOW THIS PLAGUE STARTED, BUT MY TEAM'S ALREADY BEGUN COMPARATIVE ANALYSIS.
WE'VE BEEN LOOKING AT NATURALLY OCCURRING VIRUS MUTAGENS AS WELL AS SPONGIFORM ENCEPHALOPATHIES...
...POSSIBLY CREUTZFELDT-JAKOB DISEASE OR KURU; PERHAPS FATAL FAMILIAL INSOMNIA OR GERSTMANN-STRAUSSLER-SCHEINKER DISEASE. WE'VE ALSO LOOKED AT TOXOPLASMA PARASITES, AND SOME COLD WAR BIOWEAPONS BASED ON THE RE-ENGINEERED DNA OF LANCET FLUKES, BECAUSE DICROCOELIUM DENDRITICUM AND EUHAPLORCHIS CALIFORNIENSIS WORK IN HARMONY WITH TOXOPLASMA. AND IF YOU GO IN THE DIRECTION OF RABIES—
—THAT OPENS UP A WHOLE NEW DOOR, BECAUSE
RABIES VIRUS IS AN RNA VIRUS,
THE ENGINEERING PIECE WOULD
ENCODE THE DNA INSTRUCTIONS
PERTUSSIS GENOME THAT WOULD
TEMPLATE FOR THE RABIES VIRUS
ALONG WITH AN ENZYME THAT
ACTUALLY TRANSLATE BLAH
BLAH BLAH BLAH BLAH BLAH BLAH
BLAH BLAH BLAH BLAH BLAH BLAH BLAH
WHEW!
ALL THINGS CONSIDERED, LISA... THAT REALLY WASN'T TOO BAD. I THINK WE'RE...
SPLUT

AAAHH!
CTSHH
A BAD DAY CAN ALWAYS GET A WHOLE LOT FUCKING WORSE.
OR MAYBE IT'S JUST THAT GOD HATES US. HE ADMITS HE'S COME IN LAST IN THE COSMIC SCIENCE FAIR, AND HE'S GIVING THE FUCK UP. ON THE WORLD. ON US. ON ALL OF IT.
THE HELL YOU DOING?
THOSE ARE *OUR* PEOPLE.
YOU OUT OF YOUR FUCKING *MIND?* WE HAVE TO GET HARRIET OUT OF HERE.

FUCK YOU IF YOU DON'T WANT TO HELP.
I NEVER SHOULD HAVE PULLED YOUR NARROW-ASS OUT OF THAT GRAVE.
WHAT'S THIS SHIT, SHAWN?
THIS SHIT IS THE SAME SHIT WE'VE BEEN RUNNING FROM. RIGHT BEFORE THE LOCAL NEWS STATION WENT DOWN, THEY WERE TELLING EVERYBODY THAT THE CDC HAD A CURE.
ALL I TOLD THE REPORTER WAS THAT THERE WAS HOPE. BUT WHEN THEY WENT ON THE AIR THEY LIED. THEY SAID IT WAS AN ACTUAL CURE. AND WE HAD IT.
SO EVERY-FUCKING-BODY WANTS HARRIET. EITHER TO HAVE, OR TO SELL.
BUT WE DON'T *HAVE* THE CURE, YET!
KA-BLAM
LIKE THAT MATTERS. MOST OF WHAT THE NEWS HAS BEEN SAYING IS BULLSHIT. CLOSED RESCUE CENTERS. RADIATION FROM SOME DAMN SPACE PROBE. THEY'RE JUST TALKING TO KEEP PEOPLE LISTENING.
WE TRIED TO TELL THESE ASSHOLES.
KA-BLAM KA-BLAM
POK
POK POK
POK
SO I SEE. VERY EFFECTIVE. YOU SHOULD RUN FOR OFFICE.
FUCK YOU.
BLAM

LISTEN TO ME!
THIS DOESN'T HAVE TO BE LIKE THIS. ALL WE WANT IS DR. JAYNE. GIVE HER UP AND WE'LL GO AWAY.
WHY WON'T YOU LISTEN? WE DON'T HAVE A CURE YET!
THAT'S NOT WHAT THE NEWS SAID.
YOU HAVE TO LET US GO. WE NEED TO GET TO THE LAB SO WE CAN FINISH OUR WORK.
YOU MEAN SO YOU CAN SHARE THE CURE ONLY WITH THE ENTITLED FEW. SORRY, BUT WE'VE HAD TO SWALLOW THOSE LIES FOR TOO MANY YEARS.
YOU'RE INSANE. YOU'RE ENDANGERING EVERYONE LIKE THIS. YOU SHOULD BE HELPING GET US TO THE LAB INSTEAD OF DOING THIS.
YOU KILLED MY TEAM, YOU MANIACS! YOU ALMOST KILLED ME. ARE YOU TRYING TO COMMIT SUICIDE?
YOU'RE WORSE THAN THOSE DAMN GHOULS.
THERE IS A GLOBAL CONSPIRACY THAT'S KEPT ALL OF THIS KIND OF THING FROM US. A CURE FOR CANCER. CLEAN, RENEWABLE ZERO-POINT ENERGY. BASES ON THE MOON. CALORIE-FREE CHOCOLATE. ALL OF IT.
THEY MAKE IT FOR THEMSELVES. THEY KEEP IT TO THEMSELVES. THEY'VE BEEN TURNING US INTO A MINDLESS SLAVE RACE. CHEMTRAILS. FLUORIDE IN THE WATER. IMPLANTS IN OUR HEADS.
AND LOOK WHAT'S HAPPENED! YOU BASTARDS GOT WHAT YOU WANTED, AND YOU'RE KEEPING THE CURE TO YOURSELVES.

NONE OF THAT IS TRUE. YOU KNOW IT'S NOT. IT'S ALL CONSPIRACY THEORY NONSENSE.
LOOK... LOOK... I GET THAT YOU DON'T TRUST THE GOVERNMENT. I DON'T, EITHER. I DON'T TRUST CORPORATE AMERICA, EITHER.
BUT THAT'S NOT WHO I AM. IT'S NOT WHO WE ARE.
YOU'D SAY. YOUR SCRIPT WAS WRITTEN BEFORE THE MASONS AND ILLUMINATI FOUNDED THIS COUNTRY.
YOU'RE TELLING LIE
BECAUSE THAT'S THE
WAY YOU KNOW HOW TO T
WOULD CAUSE YOU TO B
FROM THE PORES TO T
THE TRUTH.
IF 'TRUTH'
A CONCEPT
EVEN GRA
SO, SORRY IF I DON'T BELIEVE YOU, DR. JAYNE. I KNOW THE TRUTH. WE KNOW THE TRUTH, AND WE WANT THE CURE.
AND YOU DON'T WANT TO KNOW WHAT WILL HAPPEN TO YOU IF YOU MAKE US COME AND TAKE IT.
OH DEAR ME NO, YOU DON'T WANT US TO HAVE TO FORCE IT OUT OF YOU.
FUCK THIS.

REASON WITH PEOPLE LIKE THAT.
ONLY ONE WAY I KNOW OF TO DEAL WITH THEM.
2ND AMMENDMENT, YEAH. WE GOT 'EM OUTMANNED AND OUTGUNNED. WHY ARE WE EVEN HAVING THIS CONVERSATION?
MAYBE YOU GENIUSES DIDN'T NOTICE, BUT THEY HAVE A *TANK.*
AND THE BARREL IS TIED DOWN AND FACING THE WRONG WAY.
WE HAVE THE NUMBERS. LET'S JUST RUSH THE FUCKERS.
WE'D LOSE A LOT OF PEOPLE.
THIS IS WAR. SOLDIERS DIE.
THEY STARTED THIS BY KEEPING THE CURE TO THEMSELVES.
BESIDES, MARTYRS ARE USEFUL. ESPECIALLY FOR A RIGHTEOUS CAUSE.
CAN YOU SEE WHAT'S GOING ON? WHY AREN'T THEY SAYING ANYTHING?
WHATEVER THOSE FUCKTARDS ARE DOING, WE AIN'T GOING TO LIKE IT.

LAST CHANCE TO DO THE RIGHT THING!
HEY! HERE'S OUR ANSWER...
FUCK YOU, THE HORSE YOU RODE IN ON, YOUR MOTHER, YOUR UGLY STEPCHILDREN, YOUR PET DOG, YOUR GRANNY, AND EVERYONE YOU EVER MET.
FIRE! THEY CAN'T STAND AGAINST US.
FOR THE CURE! FOR THE CURE!
SURPRISE, MOTHERFUCKERS.
BUDA-BUDA-BUDA-BUDA-BUDA

...OH GOD...
I GOT THE SONS OF BITCHES. DID YOU SEE THAT? I...
SOB

YEAH. SO THAT'S WHAT WINNING LOOKS LIKE.
THIS IS WHAT SURVIVAL OF THE SPECIES LOOKS LIKE.
THIS IS THE VIEW FROM THE MORAL HIGH GROUND.
GOD HELP US.
AT LEAST THE WORST IS BEHIND US...
WHOA, WHOA, SLOW DOWN. WHAT'S THAT?
OH... SHIT...
DADDY'S GONNA ROCK...
DADDY'S GONNA ROLL...

ART BY
DREW MOSS
COLORS BY
JAY FOTOS
BADDOG

HERE'S THE SKINNY. THE DEAD ROSE—A DISEASE OR RADIATION OR SOME SHIT. POINT IS, THEY STOPPED BEING DEAD DEAD AND BECAME WALKING AND BITING DEAD.
WHEN THAT HAPPENED, EVERYBODY TOTALLY LOST THEIR SHIT.
A BUNCH OF SCIENCE NERDS THINK THEY MAY BE ON THE VERGE OF A CURE. BUT SOME FUCKTARD REPORTER WENT ON AIR TO SAY THERE WAS A CURE.
DR. HARRIET JAYNE IS THE LAST OF THE CDC RESEARCH TEAM LEFT ALIVE. THE ONLY CHANCE WE HAVE—AND BY WE, I MEAN THE WHOLE HUMAN FUCKING RACE—IS FOR ME TO GET HER TO A RESEARCH STATION ON WOLFE ISLAND IN ONTARIO.
AND THESE FINE UPSTANDING MEMBERS OF SOCIETY WANT TO KIDNAP HER TO GET THE CURE FOR THEMSELVES, AND THEN SET THEMSELVES UP AS THE EXCLUSIVE DISTRIBUTORS OF SURVIVAL.
MAKES ME EMBARRASSED TO BE A CARBON-BASED LIFE FORM.
WELL, FUCK ME BLIND AND MOVE THE FURNITURE.
HAS EVERYONE GONE CERTIFIABLY INSANE?
CLEARLY.
JESUS H. T. CHRIST...
...ON A SKATEBOARD.

GIVE US THE SCIENCE NERD!
GIVE US THE BITCH WITH THE BRAINS!
OH, GREAT. A PACK OF SEXIST JACKASSES.
REALLY? THAT'S YOUR BIG TAKEAWAY FROM THIS MOMENT?
IF IT AIN'T ONE GODDAMN THING, IT'S ANOTHER.
WOULD HAVE BEEN BETTER OFF GETTING CHOMPED WITH MY CREW.
FUCKITY-FUCK-FUCK.
WE NEED THE LADY DOCTOR.
WHAT ABOUT THE OTHER PEOPLE?
I DON'T SEE NOBODY ELSE.
ALL I SEE IS LUNCH FOR BERT AND ERNIE.
DADDY'S GONNA ROCK...
...DADDY'S GONNA ROLL.

GOT ONE CHANCE TO SAVE THE WORLD. BE A HERO. REDEEM MY SORRY ASS. GET HARRIET TO THE LAB ON WOLFE LAKE. EASY AS SHIT.
I MEAN... ZOMBIES CAN'T EAT THROUGH A TANK. PIECE OF FUCKING CAKE, RIGHT?
WRONG.
ASSHOLE REPORTER GOES AND SAYS WE ALREADY HAVE A CURE. NOW EVERY DIPSHIT WITH WHEELS AND A GUN WANTS TO PISS IN THE DAMN PUNCH BOWL.
VRRRRRRRRRRR

THESE IDIOTS WANT TO MAKE A FIGHT OF IT? SURE. FINE. WHY NOT? THEY GOT BIKES. THEY HAVE NUMBERS. THEY'RE PACKING LOTS OF GUNS. EVEN GOT SOME ZOMBIES ON LEASHES.
YEAH. GOING TO HAVE TO PROCESS THAT LATER. ZOMBIES ON LEASHES.
BUT LET'S SEE WHAT THEY THINK WHEN I SHOVE AN AMP ROUND SET FOR AIRBURST UP THEIR ASSES.
BA-BOOOOOOOOM!

ONLY SAW ONE COCKSUCKER GO INTO THAT TANK. HE CAN'T RELOAD FAST.
RUSH THEM! GET THAT WOMAN!

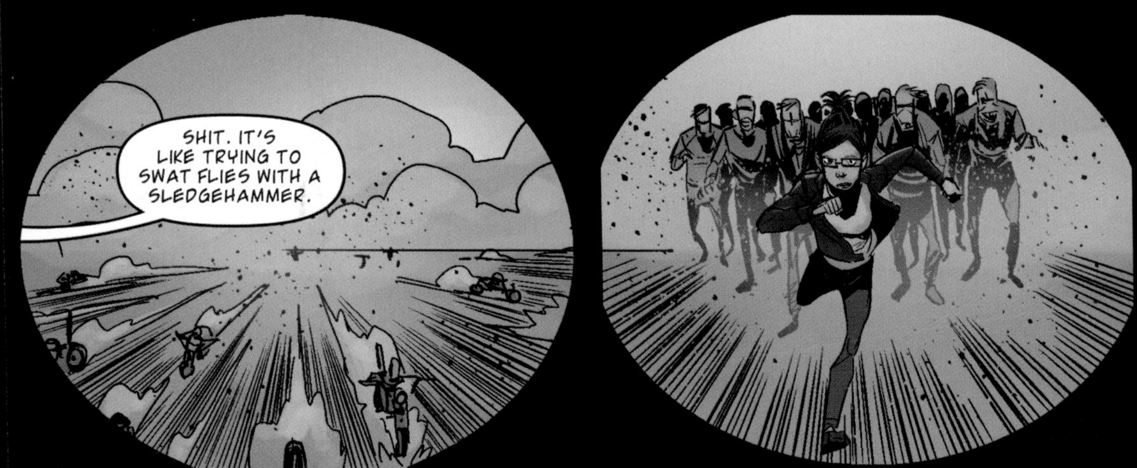
SHIT. IT'S LIKE TRYING TO SWAT FLIES WITH A SLEDGEHAMMER.

STREINER QUARRY
OWW!
YEAH, SURPRISE, SURPRISE, ASSHOLE.
OH. CRAP.

RRRRRR-RRROOOOOOMMMMMMM
KER-SPLUTTTTT
KREEEEEEEEE

HOPE YOU DON'T MIND IF I CRASH YOUR PARTY, MA'AM. BUT IT LOOKED LIKE TOO MUCH FUN TO SIT OUT.
I... UM... OKAY?

STAY BACK! WE GOT THIS SHIT.
STEP OFF, YOU FAT OLD FUCK. WE JUST WANT THE WOMAN. YOU CAN STILL WALK AWAY.
DIDN'T YOUR MAMA EVER TELL YOU NOT TO BRING A GUN TO A BAT FIGHT?
BESIDES, WHY YOU BOYS WANT A SCIENTIST FOR, ANYWAY? THERE'S NO VACCINE FOR STUPID!
CRACK
WHO ARE YOU, AND HOW DO YOU KNOW I'M A—
YOU'RE ALL OVER THE NEWS, KIDDO.
YOU'RE PROBABLY THE MOST FAMOUS PERSON ON EARTH. THERE'S YOU, AND THEN GOD, AND THEN, I DUNNO, MAYBE SCARLETT JOHANSSON.
BUT *YOU'RE* THE CAT'S ASS. YOU'RE WORTH *MY* WEIGHT IN GOLD.
WHICH IS WHY THESE GENIUSES ARE WILLING TO DIE TO GRAB YOU.

NO! HE'S ON OUR SIDE.

THIS IS ROUND ONE, MOTHERFUCKERS. GO DO YOUR HAPPY DANCE AND SING KUMBAYA.
BUT WE GOT YOUR NUMBER NOW!

YEAH, YOU DO. THE NUMBER IS US ONE AND YOU FUCK-ALL!

CONVENTIONAL WISDOM SHOULD TELL US THAT A BLAST FROM A TANK...
...SHOULD BE ENOUGH TO SETTLE THE HASH OF YOUR STANDARD BUNCH OF SOCIAL MISFITS ON MOTOR BIKES.
BUT LET'S FACE IT, KIDS—TIMES HAVE CHANGED.

DOC... I MEAN HARRIET... YOU CAN STOP THIS, RIGHT? I MEAN THERE'S A REAL CHANCE.
I CAN TRY.

AND BY 'TRY' YOU MEAN YOU CAN ACTUALLY DO THIS?
'CAUSE THAT IS WHAT THEY'RE SAYING ON THE NEWS. YOU'RE GOING TO SAVE THE WORLD.

I WISH.
CRAP. SOUNDS LIKE THERE'S A STORY NEEDS LISTENING TO, BUT FIRST WE HAVE SOME WORK TO DO.

I CAN DO MY PART. I'M NOT FRAGILE, YOU KNOW.
YOU'RE FIERCE AS SHIT, DOC, BUT YOUR *PART* IS STAYING SAFE AND ALIVE.
MINNIE WAS IN H.R. FOR THE CDC. DIEGO WAS IN I.T. AT CNN.
VIOLA WORKED FOR THE IRS, BUT SHE'S OKAY.
DEE'S MY NEIGHBOR. AND MR. MAN-BUN HERE'S MY NEPHEW, JAKE.
AS FOR ME? I'M A WRITER. I'M NOT STEPHEN KING, BUT I DID OKAY. KIND OF TOM WAITS MEETS JOE LANSDALE, WITH A BIT OF THE BIG LEBOWSKI THROWN IN FOR COLOR.
...KID HERE KIND OF NEEDS YOUR HELP.
IT'S NOTHING. BARELY BROKE THE SKIN.
LISTEN TO ME, JAKE... THIS IS SERIOUS. YOU'RE INFECTED.
BULLSHIT. THAT'S JUST WHAT THEY'RE SAYING ON THE NET TO SCARE PEOPLE. IT'S JUST A LITTLE BITE.
I WISH THAT WAS TRUE, JAKE. I REALLY DO.

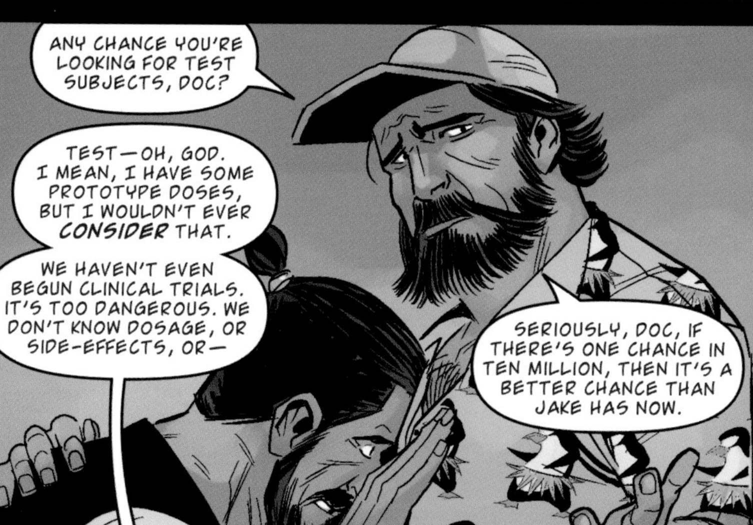
ANY CHANCE YOU'RE LOOKING FOR TEST SUBJECTS, DOC?
TEST—OH, GOD. I MEAN, I HAVE SOME PROTOTYPE DOSES, BUT I WOULDN'T EVER CONSIDER THAT.
WE HAVEN'T EVEN BEGUN CLINICAL TRIALS. IT'S TOO DANGEROUS. WE DON'T KNOW DOSAGE, OR SIDE-EFFECTS, OR—
SERIOUSLY, DOC, IF THERE'S ONE CHANCE IN TEN MILLION, THEN IT'S A BETTER CHANCE THAN JAKE HAS NOW.

I DON'T WANT TO DIE.
I HAVEN'T EVEN BEEN TO PARIS YET.

PRETTY SURE EVERYONE IN PARIS IS EATING EACH OTHER, TOO.
HUSH, SON. KID'S HAVING A MOMENT HERE.

EVEN IF I WERE TO AGREE, THE VACCINE IS DESIGNED TO WORK ON LATE STAGE INFECTIONS OR FULLY TRANSITIONED CASES. I COULDN'T EVEN TRY UNTIL...

GOD... PLEASE!

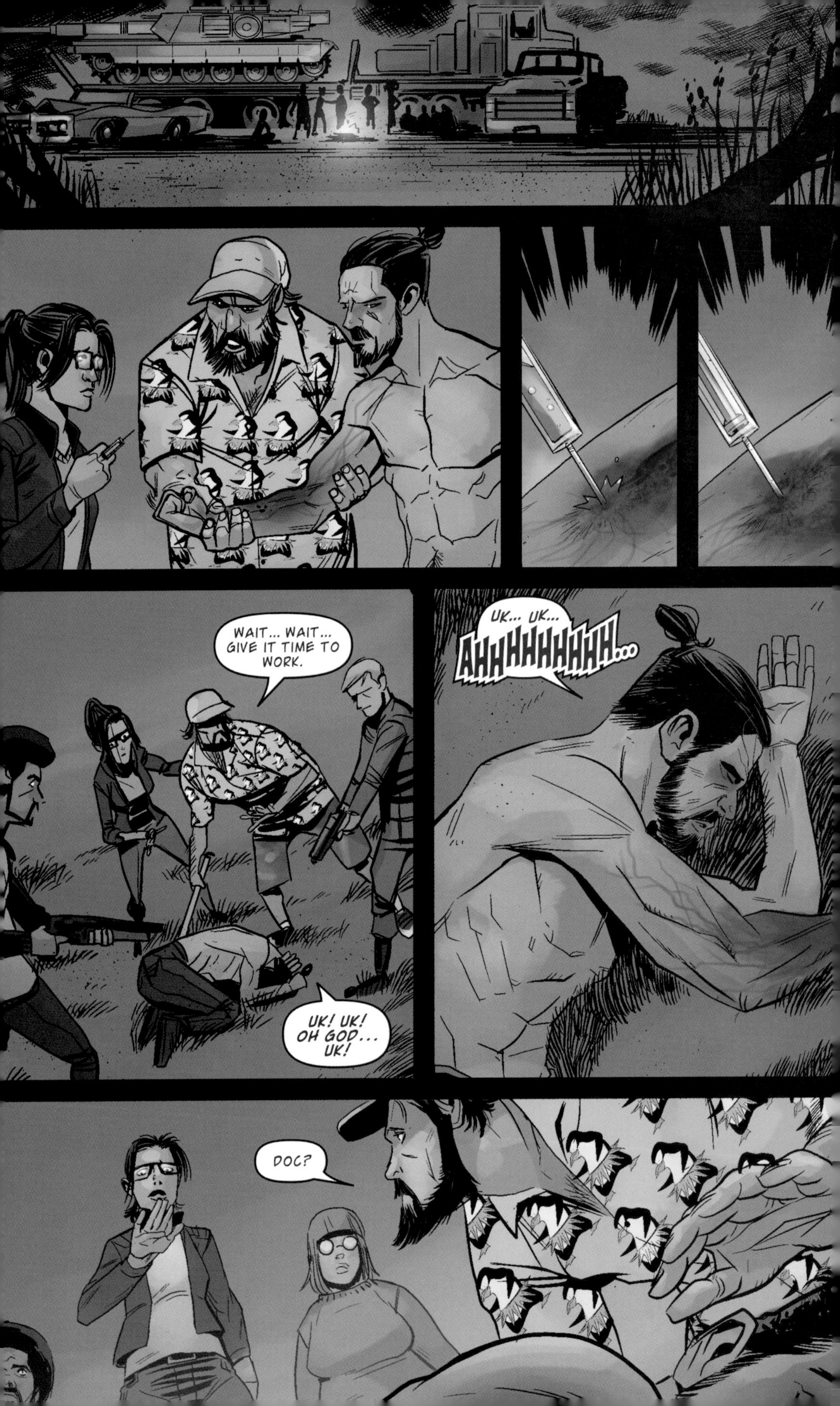
WAIT... WAIT... GIVE IT TIME TO WORK.
UK! UK! OH GOD... UK!
UK... UK...
AHHHHHHHHH...
DOC?

JAKE?
KID... ARE YOU IN THERE?
C'MON, KID, GIVE ME A HAPPY ENDING HERE.
GAAHHHHHH!
GOD ALMIGHTY.

HE KILLED HIMSELF. WHAT DOES THAT EVEN MEAN?
IS THAT WHAT YOU WANTED TO HAPPEN?
NO. NO... BUT... OH GOD. HE DIDN'T ATTACK ANYONE.
HE DIDN'T TRY TO BITE ANYONE...
OH MY GOD... I THINK THE VACCINE WORKS...

I'M SO SORRY THAT I COULDN'T SAVE YOUR NEPHEW, THOUGH.
YOU DID SAVE HIM, DOC. WITHOUT THAT VACCINE, HE'D HAVE BEEN A MONSTER. HE'D HAVE KILLED US OR MADE US KILL HIM.
INSTEAD, HE HAD ENOUGH OF HIMSELF LEFT TO MAKE A BRAVE CHOICE. HE DECIDED TO KILL HIMSELF RATHER THAN BE A MONSTER.
YOU'RE A GODDAMN HERO, DOC. YOU'RE GOING TO SAVE THE WORLD.

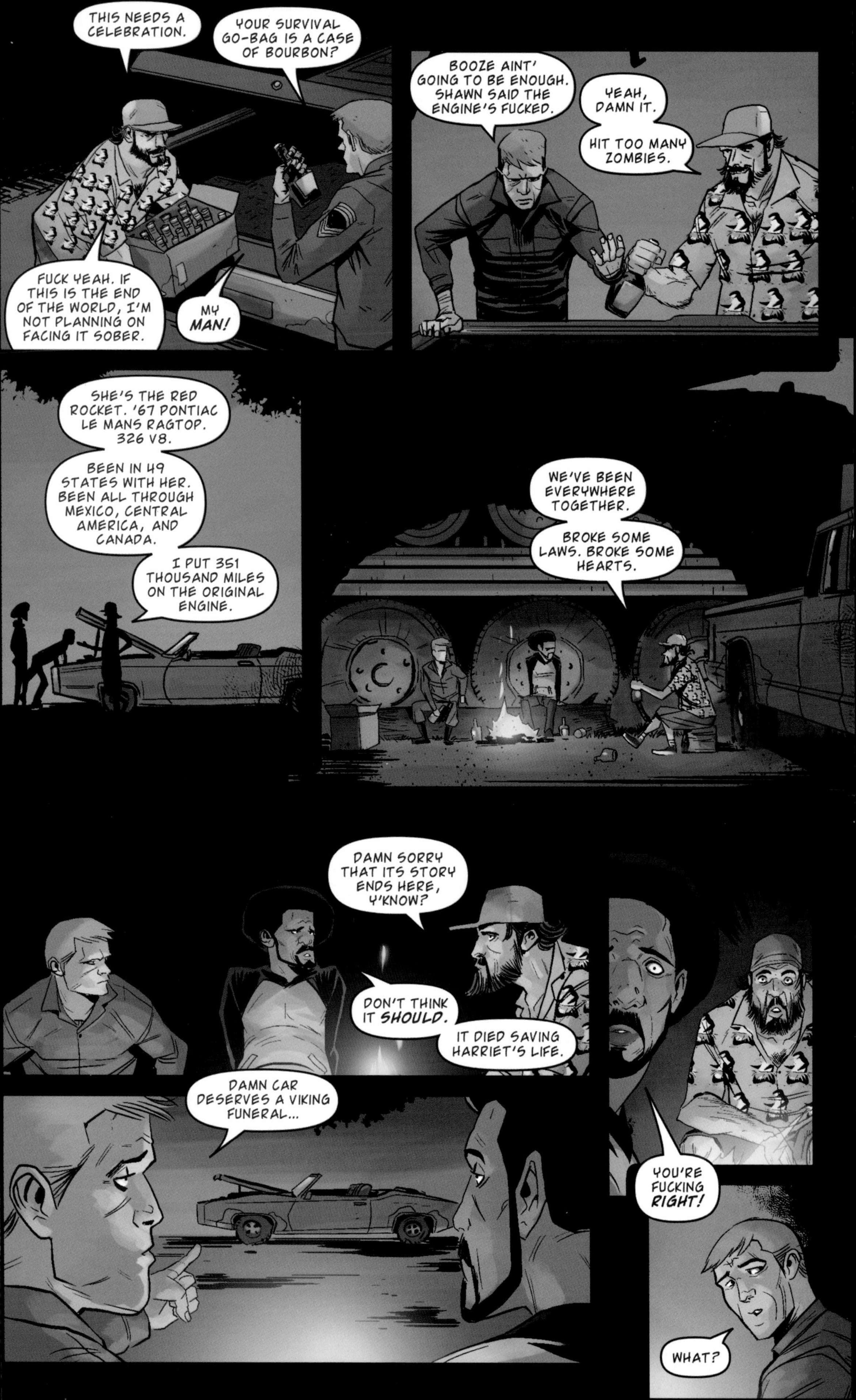
THIS NEEDS A CELEBRATION.
YOUR SURVIVAL GO-BAG IS A CASE OF BOURBON?
FUCK YEAH. IF THIS IS THE END OF THE WORLD, I'M NOT PLANNING ON FACING IT SOBER.
MY **MAN!**
BOOZE AINT' GOING TO BE ENOUGH. SHAWN SAID THE ENGINE'S FUCKED.
YEAH, DAMN IT.
HIT TOO MANY ZOMBIES.
SHE'S THE RED ROCKET. '67 PONTIAC LE MANS RAGTOP. 326 V8.
BEEN IN 49 STATES WITH HER. BEEN ALL THROUGH MEXICO, CENTRAL AMERICA, AND CANADA.
I PUT 351 THOUSAND MILES ON THE ORIGINAL ENGINE.
WE'VE BEEN EVERYWHERE TOGETHER.
BROKE SOME LAWS. BROKE SOME HEARTS.
DAMN SORRY THAT ITS STORY ENDS HERE, Y'KNOW?
DON'T THINK IT **SHOULD.**
IT DIED SAVING HARRIET'S LIFE.
DAMN CAR DESERVES A VIKING FUNERAL...
YOU'RE FUCKING **RIGHT!**
WHAT?

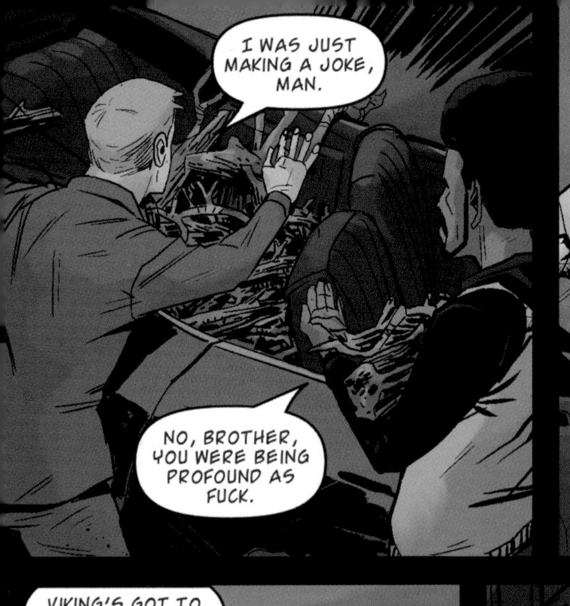
I WAS JUST MAKING A JOKE, MAN.
NO, BROTHER, YOU WERE BEING PROFOUND AS FUCK.

VIKING'S GOT TO HAVE A SERVANT IN VALHALLA.

NEEDS WEAPONS, TOO.
I'VE GOT FIRE!

MIGHT NOT BE THE RIGHT TIME TO ASK, BUT IS THERE STILL GAS IN THE TANK?

OH FUCK FUCK FUCK FUCK—

PUSH FASTER!

WAH-HOOOOOOOOOOOO

WHAT'S HAPPENING? ARE THE BIKERS BACK?

UMMMM...
LET ME GET THIS STRAIGHT.
YOU THREE OVERGROWN JUVENILE DELINQUENTS GAVE A VIKING FUNERAL TO A MUSCLE CAR?

WELL...
...YEAH. KIND OF...
...SEEMED LIKE THE BEST THING TO DO AT THE TIME...

YOU IDIOTS ARE AWARE THAT THIS IS THE APOCALYPSE, RIGHT?
ACTUAL END OF DAYS.
HALF THE PEOPLE IN AMERICA ARE REANIMATED CORPSES TRYING TO EAT US.
THE OTHER HALF ARE PSYCHOS TRYING TO KILL ***YOU*** AND CAPTURE ***ME.***
AND YOU IDIOTS RESPOND TO ALL THIS BY GETTING DRUNK AND SETTING YOUR CAR ON FIRE?
TECHNICALLY, DOC, WE ARE ***NOT*** DRUNK. WE ARE, IN FACT, ***SHIT-FACED.*** IT'S A WHOLE 'NOTHER LEVEL.
SHAWN'S RIGHT. WE ARE TOTALLY FIT-SHACED.
TOTALLY.
DID YOU AT LEAST BRING ENOUGH FOR EVERYONE?

GRRRRRRRRRRRRRRRRRRR

BAD DOG

ART BY
DREW MOSS
COLORS BY
JAY FOTOS

ZOMBIES! FUCK!
HOLY SHIT!

DOC, GET BACK!
I CAN FIGHT, DAMN IT!
YOU CAN DIE, TOO, AND THEN WHERE WOULD WE BE?

TANK-BOY'S RIGHT, DOC. EVERY ONE OF US POOR SONS'A'BITCHES IS EXPENDABLE 'CEPT YOU.
KA-SPLOOOOK

DIEGO—
WATCH! AHHHH...
SHIT!
AY DIOS MIO!
AIIEEEEE!
KRUNNCHHHH
OH, WHAT, YOU THINK BLERDS ARE ALL TALK AND NO BITE? DEAL WITH THAT SHIT!
LANGUAGE, DEE! OH—DEAR!
GET TO SHELTER.
IS HARRIET SAFE?
SHE'S... UM... FINE.

DIEGO! GET YOUR SKINNY ASS OVER HERE!
DOC! WE NEED SOME OF YOUR CURE. DIEGO'S BEEN BIT!
I KEEP TELLING EVERYONE— IT'S NOT A DAMN CURE!
I DON'T CARE IF IT'S VIAGRA, DAMN IT, HE'S TURNING!
I ONLY HAVE THREE DOSES LEFT!
STOP PUSHING ME!
HEY, FLORENCE NIGHTINGALE—GET IN THE FUCKING TRUCK!

KILL... ME...

AH, FUCK.
KA-BLAM
DAMN, BROTHER. YOU DESERVED BETTER.

DADDY? YEAH... I FOUND 'EM.

THIS IS HOW IT IS NOW. EVERYWHERE IS A TRAP. EVERYONE IS AN ENEMY. EACH OF US IS A TRAITOR TO THE LIVING THE SECOND WE DIE.
TEN THOUSAND YEARS OF HUMAN CIVILIZATION. EVERYTHING WE LEARNED, EVERYTHING WE BUILT, ALL WE KNOW ABOUT THE WORLD AND THE UNIVERSE. AND NOW THE ONLY THING THAT DEFINES US IS WHETHER WE'RE PREDATORS OR PREY.
NO DIGNITY LEFT. HOPE AND OPTIMISM ARE GETTING BITCH-SLAPPED. COMPASSION'S LYING DEAD IN A DITCH SOMEWHERE.
LISTEN TO ME FOR A SECOND, WILL YOU?
WE COULDN'T HAVE SAVED DIEGO. BEST CASE WAS THAT THE SERUM GAVE HIM THE OPTION OF THROWING HIMSELF OFF THE CLIFF LIKE JAKE DID LAST NIGHT.
WE CAN'T BEAT OURSELVES UP OVER THAT. HARRIET'S RIGHT, THIS ISN'T A CURE.
MAYBE.
WHAT DO YOU MEAN 'MAYBE'?
ALL WE KNOW ABOUT THE CURRENT VERSION OF THE SERUM IS WHAT HAPPENED TO JAKE.
THAT'S ONE CASE, ONE REACTION. WHO KNOWS WHAT WOULD HAVE HAPPENED TO DIEGO. OR ANYONE ELSE.
EVERYONE IS DIFFERENT. I NEED TO DO A **LOT** MORE TRIALS, AND UNDER CLINICAL CONDITIONS.
WE'D ONLY BEGUN TESTING TO OBSERVE THE EFFECTS IF GIVEN **BEFORE** INFECTION.
OR AFTER NATURAL DEATH. OR AFTER REANIMATION. THERE ARE SO MANY VARIABLES...
BEFORE INFECTION?
SURE. THE PREMISE IS THAT TECHNICALLY **EVERYONE** IS ALREADY INFECTED. NOTHING ELSE WOULD EXPLAIN WHY ALL RECENT DEAD COME BACK.
BITES DON'T SPREAD THE DISEASE, BUT THEY POSSESS A SECONDARY PATHOGEN THAT CAUSES A RAPID NATURAL DEATH. THE WHOLE THING OPERATES MORE LIKE A PARASITE THAN A DISEASE.
WE BELIEVE THIS IS A MUTATED VERSION OF SOME KIND OF BIOWEAPON THAT SOMEHOW GOT RELEASED. MAYBE **SEIF AL DIN**, OR **LUCIFER 113**, OR **VIJIVSHIT ODIN-VASEMNATZETS**.
ONE CLINICAL MODEL WE WANTED TO TRY WAS TO PRE-INJECT EVERYONE, SO THAT IF THEY WERE BITTEN THEIR SYSTEMS WOULD BE READY TO COMBAT THE PSYCHOCHEMICAL CHANGES.
WHICH MEANS THEY'D BE WHAT? STILL ALIVE? OR HALF-ALIVE? HALF-ZOMS? WOULD THEY RETAIN THEIR INTELLIGENCE AND MEMORIES?
WE DON'T KNOW, BUT THAT'S THE HOPE. IF WE CAN PRESERVE THE HIGHER BRAIN FUNCTIONS, WE MIGHT BE ABLE TO STOP THE CYCLE OF AGGRESSION.
SURE, BUT THEY'D STILL BE FUCKING ZOMBIES.
YES, BUT WE'D HAVE MORE TIME TO WORK ON A PERMANENT CURE.

A PERMANENT CURE. JESUS CHRIST. AND I THOUGHT WE WERE DONE. I THOUGHT THIS WAS THE WHOLE FOUR HORSEMEN AND CURTAINS DOWN THING.
TELL YOU WHAT, DOC... IF YOU'RE LOOKING FOR VOLUNTEERS...
GOD, NO! WE HAVEN'T TESTED IT ON A HEALTHY LIVING PERSON YET. ONLY ON LAB ANIMALS, AND THE RESULTS WERE ALL OVER THE PLACE.
SOME DIED AND REANIMATED EVEN FASTER. SOME WERE AGGRESSIVE VECTORS WITH GREATER CUNNING BUT NO TRACE OF HUMAN PERSONALITY.
ANY OF THEM KEEP THEIR SHIT TOGETHER?
NOT ENOUGH TO RISK IT. NOT WITH YOU TWO.
FOR THE RECORD I DIDN'T ACTUALLY VOLUNTEER...
WHAT WE REALLY NEED TO DO, UYS, IS GET ME AND MY RESEARCH TO WOLFE LAKE. GENERAL COPPERHEAD HAS A LAB WAITING, AND I'M READY TO JUMP RIGHT IN.
EVEN THOUGH THE SERUM I HAVE ISN'T A CURE YET, I THINK I'M ON THE VERGE OF CREATING ONE.
THEN BELIEVE ME, DOC, WE ARE GOING TO GET YOU THERE.
YOU KNOW THAT'S RIGHT. NOTHING AND NOBODY'S GOING TO STOP US.
URKKKK
WELL, FUCK ME TO TEARS AND CALL IT LOVE STORY.
CLUNKITY-CLUNK-CLUNK-HSSSSSSSS

CAN YOU FIX IT?
SURE. IN A SHOP. WITH A CHAIN HOIST AND A NEW ENGINE BLOCK. AND NEW VALVES. COUPLE OF GASKETS. SOME HOSES...
FUUUUUUCK...
WAIT, SO THIS BIG DUMPSTER ON WHEELS CAN ONLY GO 45 MILES AN HOUR ON A PAVED ROAD. AND AFTER 250, SHE RUNS DRY?
AS A BONE.
WOLFE ISLAND'S LIKE... 453 MILES FROM HERE.
WE CAN STOP TO REFUEL.
WHILE FIGHTING OFF A BAZILLION ZOMBIES AND A BUNCH OF ASSHOLES ON HARLEYS?
I AM NOT NEARLY HIGH ENOUGH FOR THIS SHIT.
COULD BE WORSE.
WE COULD BE DOING THIS WITHOUT A FUCKING TANK.

CORRECT ME IF I'M WRONG, BUT THAT WAS A SMIDGE UNDER 200 MILES.
A SMIDGE.
LIKE 175.
A SMIDGE-AND-A-HALF. SHE'S OLD AND FAT, BUT SHE'LL MAKE IT.
GUYS! THERE ARE SOME INFECTED COMING.
HOW MANY?
UM... PRETTY MUCH ALL OF THEM.
THERE'S SO MANY. WHAT ARE WE GOING TO DO?
TANK.
TANK.
HELL YEAH, TANK.

EVERYTHING I SAID ABOUT THIS FAT, OLD GIRL.
BIKER MOTHERFUCKERS TRY SOMETHING NOW. SPEAKING OF FATTIES, YOU GOING TO HAND THAT SCOOBY DOOBIE OVER HERE OR NOT?
HOW MANY OF THESE YOU GOT?
NOT ENOUGH TO MAKE SENSE OF THE WORLD, BROTHER. SPEAKING OF WHICH—
JUST BETWEEN YOU AND ME AND THE BIG WIDE OPEN... WHAT DO YOU THINK ABOUT THIS SERUM? YOU SAW WHAT HAPPENED TO MY NEPHEW. YOUR GUT TELLING YOU ANYTHING ABOUT OUR CHANCES HERE?
SHIT, KAHUNA, I DON'T KNOW. I REALLY DON'T. BUT I'LL TELL YOU THIS MUCH...
...I GOT NOTHING LEFT TO BELIEVE IN BUT HARRIET'S MAGIC POTION. FAMILY'S DEAD. FRIENDS ARE DEAD. WORLD'S COUGHING UP BLOOD. GOVERNMENT CRAWLED UP ITS OWN ASS AND GOD'S SENDING ALL OUR PRAYERS DIRECT TO VOICEMAIL.
SO IF THERE'S EVEN A SNOWBALL'S CHANCE THAT HARRIET'S ONTO SOMETHING, THEN I'LL WALK RIGHT UP TO THE GATES OF HELL AND KICK THE DEVIL IN HIS BIG, RED DICK.
YUP. PRETTY MUCH HOW I SEE THINGS.
BETTER TO BURN OUT THAN FADE AWAY.
I *HEARD* THAT.

WOLFE ISLAND
24.4 MILES
LIMERICK VETERINARY CLINIC
I... I CAN'T BELIEVE IT. WE DID IT. WE GOT HERE.
I TOLD YOU WE WOULD, DOC.
WE WOULD NEVER HAD MADE IT THIS FAR WITHOUT YOU. YOU DO REALIZE THAT, DON'T YOU? YOU'RE KIND OF AMAZING.
I... UM... SAY, DOC... WHAT ARE YOU DOING AFTER THE APOCALYPSE?
I—
HEY, BEFORE YOU TWO POP EACH OTHER'S CHERRIES, MAYBE YOU BETTER COME UP AND TAKE A LOOK AT THIS.

CHRIST.
NOW WHAT?

IT'S PROBABLY THE TANK. NOISY AS HELL. IT'S DRAWING THEM.
OH MY GOD.
IT'S NOT YOUR FAULT.
I'M NOT SURE HOW MUCH MORE OF THIS SHIT I CAN TAKE.
WE'RE ALMOST TO THE ISLAND. IF WE HAVE TO FIGHT OUR WAY THROUGH, THEN WE'LL FIGHT.
FUCK YEAH.
LANGUAGE, DEAR. HECK YES IS MORE APPROPRIATE.
I DON'T KNOW IF I'M DOING THIS RIGHT!
ARE WE GOING FORWARD?
Y-YES.
YOU'RE DOING IT RIGHT. PEDAL TO THE METAL.

CHRIST, SHAWN— I THINK THERE'S ANOTHER SWARM OVER THERE.

WELL, FUCK ME YELLOW AND CALL ME A BANANA.

SO... OKAY. MONSTER TRUCKS.
FIRST IT WAS ZOMBIES. THEN BIKERS. THEN BIKERS WITH ZOMBIES.
NOW, IT'S MONSTER TRUCKS. WITH MACHINE GUNS.
GET THE SCIENCE GEEK. EVERYONE ELSE DIES. DO IT!
NO! DON'T LET THEM STOP US. WE'RE SO CLOSE!
NO. FUCKING. WAY.

SURE. FINE. WHATEVER. YOU WANT TO MEASURE DICKS?
I'LL SEE YOUR MONSTER TRUCKS AND RAISE YOU ONE MOTHERFUCKING M1 ABRAMS BATTLE TANK.
THIS AIN'T NORMAL. THIS AIN'T A MILE FROM NORMAL. THIS IS ALL THE WAY DOWN A CROOKED ROAD FROM NORMAL.
YOU WANT TO KILL US, YOU ASS-CLOWNS? JOKE'S ON YOU, 'CAUSE I HAVE COLON CANCER. I HAVE A CLEAR CONSCIENCE AND NOTHING TO LOSE.
I'M GOING TO DIE A VIRGIN.
I'M GOING TO DIE WITHOUT EVER GOING TO SAN DIEGO COMIC CON.
FUCK!
LANGUAGE!

DADDY'S GONNA ROCK.
DADDY'S GONNA ROLL.
THEY HAVE FREAKING RPGS! HARRIET, FLOOR IT!
I *AM* FLOORING IT. GOD. MY GRANDMOTHER WAS SLOW, BUT AT LEAST SHE WAS OLD.
DID SHE WEIGH SIXTY TONS?
ONLY AFTER SHE WENT TO WEIGHT WATCHERS.

DOWN—
DOWN!
THEY'RE EVERYWHERE!
SKRUNCHHHH
RUN, KID! GET TO THE TANK BEFORE—
POK POKPOK
—UGHHHH! FUCK!

MAN DOWN! MAN DOWN! HARRIET—SLOW THE FUCK DOWN!
CHRIST, MAN, HOW MUCH DO YOU WEIGH?
OOOOOF!

DEE! WATCH OUT— BEHIND YOU!
AIIIEEEEE!
BUDA-BUDA-BUDA-BUDA-BUDA
SPLUT
SPLUT
SPLUT
DADDY'S GONNA...
WHAAOOOOOOOM

HARRIET... UGHH... GET US OUT OF HERE... DRIVE.
BUT I...
FOR GOD'S SAKE... -COUGH-COUGH- JUST DRIVE...
WOLF LAKE FERRY

WE MADE IT, SURE, BUT WE CAN'T TAKE THIS BEAST ONTO THE FERRY. THERE ARE SOME BOATS OUT THERE. I KNOW BOATS BETTER THAN I KNOW MY OWN DICK. I CAN GET HARRIET OVER TO THE ISLAND, BUT WE'LL HAVE TO GET OUT AND MAKE A RUN FOR IT.
GONNA NEED YOU BOYS TO BUY US SOME TIME.
WAIT— WHAT? NO! WE ALL HAVE TO GO.
I DIG THE OPTIMISM, DOC, BUT LET'S FACE IT. HOMEBOY AND ME AIN'T RUNNING ANYWHERE.
-COUGH-COUGH AIN'T WALKING ANYWHERE EITHER, MAN.
THERE IS A METRIC FUCK-TON OF THEM STILL COMING. THEY'RE SCARED OF THE TANK, BUT THEY WON'T BE FOR LONG. IF WE'RE GOING, WE NEED TO GO NOW.
CAN YOU BOYS GIVE US A LITTLE COVER?
I CAN'T EVEN FEEL MY LEGS.
ME NEITHER. DOC... WE TRIED. I'M SORRY, BUT WE DID ALL WE COULD.
ALL? YOU KNOW, BROTHER, I THINK THERE'S ONE MORE THING LEFT TO TRY.
DOC... HARRIET... YOU GOT THREE DOSES LEFT...?

NO! I CAN'T. IT'S STILL UNTESTED FOR USE ON THE LIVING.
THERE'S NO WAY TO KNOW WHAT IT WOULD DO TO YOU. NO, I SIMPLY CAN'T!
IF YOU DON'T, THEN ALL FOUR OF US DIE. RIGHT HERE AND NOW.
AND IF YOU WAIT, AND SHAWN AND ME DIE AND TURN, THEN WHAT? YOU WILLING TO STAND ON THE HIPPOCRATIC OATH AND LET THE WHOLE DAMN WORLD EAT ITSELF? I MEAN, WHAT'S PLAN B HERE?
HE'S GOT A POINT. AND THE CLOCK'S TICKING. I KNOW I CAN GET YOU TO THE BOAT AND ACROSS TO THE ISLAND.
OH... GOD...
MAYBE THIS IS GOD'S PLAN.
YEAH. ALL THAT MOVING IN MYSTERIOUS WAYS SHIT.
BESIDES, NONE OF US MADE MUCH OF A DIFFERENCE IN THE WORLD. NOT ME, THAT'S FOR SURE. WE FOUGHT ALL THE WAY HERE.
IF WE'RE GOING TO DIE, THEN LET IT AT LEAST MEAN SOMETHING.

SUCKS TO PUT THIS ON YOU, DOC, BUT LIFE'S LIKE THAT.
VIKING FUNERAL, BOYS.
VIKING FUNERAL.
VIKING MOTHERFUCKING FUNERAL.

THEY'RE CLEAR.
WELL... THIS FEELS WEIRD AS FUCK.
DOESN'T HURT AT ALL. MAKES ME A LITTLE CRANKY, THOUGH.
CRANKY AS A MOTHERFUCKER.
HUNGRY, TOO.
YEAH... I COULD EAT.

WHUP-WHUP-WHUP-WHUP
WE'RE SAFE, KAHUNA. WE'RE...
SAFE...?
OH GOD... NO!

NOOOOOOOOOOOOO!

NAME IS DR. HARRIET JAYNE.
RRRRRRR... ARRGHHH... RRRRR...
PLEASE! DON'T HURT THEM! THEY'RE IMPORTANT TEST SUBJECTS.
PLEASE...
...THEY'RE IMPORTANT...
I'M A RESEARCH SCIENTIST FOR THE CDC, ON LOAN TO DARPA, AND NOW WITH THE SPECIAL RESEARCH STATION AT WOLFE LAKE.
MY TEAM AND I WERE WORKING ON A CURE FOR THE PLAGUE. OR A TREATMENT.
ON SOMETHING THAT WOULD STOP THE DEAD FROM ATTACKING AND CONSUMING THE LIVING.
...RRRRRRRR...
MY TEAM IS DEAD. MY FRIENDS ARE DEAD...
...OR LIVING DEAD.
BUT I KNOW I'M ON THE RIGHT TRACK.
HANSON AND SHAWN SAVED MY LIFE AFTER THEY WERE INJECTED.
THAT PROVES SOMETHING. THAT MEANS SOMETHING.
PEOPLE CALL THIS THE END OF THE WORLD.
I HOPE THEY'RE WRONG.
I HOPE THEY'RE WRONG...

bert

ART BY
SANTÍPEREZ
COLORS BY
JAY FOTOS

BITE ME

ART BY
SANTÍPEREZ
COLORS BY
JAY FOTOS
BITE ME

ART BY
SANTÍPEREZ
COLORS BY
JAY FOTOS

CHOKE

By Jonathan Maberry

The lieutenant said to hold it.

So we're holding it.

Chokepoint Baker: five miles up a crooked road, fifty miles from the command post, a hundred miles from the war.

They dropped us here three days after what the radio has been calling "'First Night."

Couple days later, I heard a DJ out of Philly call it "Last Night." But the news guys always do that hysterical shit. If it's going to snow, they start talking about blizzards; two guys shove each other outside a Wal-Mart, and it's rioting in the streets. Their amps are always dialed up to eleven.

Guess that sort of thing's infectious, because we got rousted and rolled before dawn's early light.

As we climbed down off the truck, Lieutenant Bell took me aside. We'd known each other for a while, and he usually called me Sally or Sal, but not that day. He was all Joe-Army. "Listen up, corporal," he told me. "The infection is contained to the west side of this river. There are two other bridges; closest is eight klicks downstream. We're spread pretty thin, so I can spare one fireteam per bridge. This one's yours."

The bridge was rusted steel that had once been painted blue, a lane of blacktop going in each direction. No tollbooth, no nothing. Pennsylvania on one side, New Jersey on the other.

"You think you can do that, Corporal?"

I grinned. "C'mon, Loot, a couple of Cub Scouts could hold that bridge with a slingshot and a wet fart."

I always cracked him up, drunk or sober, but now he just gave me the look. The officer look.

I straightened. "Yes, sir. We'll hold it."

"You are authorized to barricade this bridge. Make sure nothing gets across. Nothing and no one, do you understand?"

For what? Some dickheads rioting on the other side of the state? I wanted to laugh.

But there was something in his eyes. He lowered his voice, so it was just heard by the two of us. Everyone else was handing empty sandbags and equipment boxes down from the truck. "This is serious shit, Sally. I need you to do this."

I gave a quick right-left look to make sure no one could hear us. "The fuck's going down, man? You got the bug-eyes going on. This is a bunch of civilians going apeshit, right?"

Bell licked his lips. Real nervous, the way a scared dog does.

"You really don't know, do you?" he asked. "Haven't you been watching the news?"

"Yeah, I've seen the news."

"They aren't civilians," he said. "Not anymore."

"What does that—?"

A sergeant came hurrying over to tell us that everything was off-loaded. Bell stepped abruptly away from me and back into his officer role. "Are we clear on everything, Corporal Tucci?"

I played my part. "Yes, sir."

Bell and the sergeant climbed back into the truck and we watched its tail lights through a faint smudge of dust. My guys—all three of them—stood with me. We turned and looked at the bridge. It was rush hour on a Friday, but the road was empty. Both sides of the bridge.

"What the hell's going on?" asked Joe Bob—and yeah, his actual name on his dog tags was Joe Bob Stanton. He was a redneck mouth-breather who joined the Reserves because nobody in the civilian world was stupid enough to let him play with guns. The geniuses here decided he should be an automatic rifleman. When they handed him an M249 Squad Automatic Weapon, he almost came in his pants.

I shook my head.

"Join the Navy," said Talia. "See the world."

"That's the Navy," said Farris. "We're the National damn Guard."

"That's my point," she said.

"C'mon," I said, "let's get this shit done."

It took us four hours to fill enough sandbags to block the western approach to the bridge. Four hours. Didn't see a single car the whole time.

At first that was okay, made it easier to work.

Later, though, none of us liked how that felt.

I was the Team Leader for this gig. Corporal Salvatore Tucci, in charge because everyone else on the team was even greener than me. Army Reserves, man. I had been in technical college working on a degree in fixing air conditioners, and I was still the most educated guy on the team. Cutting-edge, 21st century Army, my ass.

A lot of the guys who enlisted were dickheads like Joe Bob.

The other two? Farris was a slacker with no G.E.D. who mopped up at a Taco Bell. They'd made him a rifleman. And our grenadier, Talia? Her arms and her thighs were a roadmap of healed-over needle scars, but she never talked about it. I think she maybe got clean and signed up to help her stay clean.

That's Fireteam Delta. Four fuck-ups who didn't have the sense to stay out of uniform or enough useful skills to be put somewhere that mattered.

And here we were, holding Checkpoint Baker and waiting for orders.

We opened some M.R.E.s and ate bad spaghetti and some watery stuff that was supposed to be cream of broccoli soup.

"Dude," said Farris, "there's a Quiznos like three miles from here. I saw it on the way in."

"So?"

"One of us could go and get something..."

"Deserting a post in a time of crisis?" murmured Talia dryly. "I think they have a rule about that."

"It's not deserting," said Farris, but he didn't push it. I think he knew what we all thought. As soon as he was around the bend in the road he'd fire up a blunt, and that's all we needed, was to have the lieutenant roll up on Farris stoned and A.W.O.L. on my watch.

I gave him my version of the look.

He grinned like a kid who'd been caught reaching in the cookie jar.

"Hey," said Talia, "somebody's coming."

And shit if we didn't all look the wrong way first. We looked up the road, the way the truck went. Then we realized Talia was looking over the sandbags.

We turned.

There was someone on the road. Not in a car. On foot, walking along the side maybe four hundred yards away.

"Civvie," said Talia. "Looks like a kid."

I took out my binoculars. They were a cheap, low-intensity pair that I'd bought myself. Still better than the 'no pair' the National Guard had issued me. The civvie kid was maybe seventeen, wearing a Philadelphia Eagles sweatshirt, jeans, and no shoes. He walked with his head down, stumbling a little. There were dark smears on his shirt, and I'd been in enough bar fights to know what blood looked like when it dried on a football jersey. There was some blood on what I could see of his face and on both hands.

"Whoever he is," I said, "someone kicked his ass."

They took turns looking.

While Talia was looking, the guy raised his head, and she screamed. Like a horror movie scream; just a kind of yelp.

"Holy shit!"

"What?" everyone asked at the same time.

"His face..."

I took the binoculars back. The guy's head was down again. He was about a hundred yards away now, coming on but not in a hurry. If he was that jacked up, then maybe he was really out of it. Maybe he got drunk and picked the wrong fight and now his head was busted and he didn't know where he was.

"What's wrong with his face?" asked Farris.

When Talia didn't answer, I lowered the binoculars and looked at her. "Tal... what was wrong with his face?"

She still didn't answer, and there was a weird light in her eyes.

"What?" I asked.

But she didn't need to answer.

Farris said, "Holy fuck!"

I whirled around. The civvie was

thirty yards away. Close enough to see him.

Close enough to see.

The kid was walking right toward the bridge, head up now. Eyes on us.

His face...

I thought it was smeared with blood.

But that wasn't it.

He didn't have a face.

Beside me, Joe Bob said, "Wha—wha—wha—?" He couldn't even finish the word.

Farris made a gagging sound. Or maybe that was me.

The civvie kid kept walking straight toward us. Twenty yards. His mouth was open, and, for a stupid minute, I thought he was speaking. But you needed lips to speak. And a tongue. All he had were teeth. The rest of the flesh on his face was—gone.

Just gone.

Torn away. Or...

Eaten away.

"Jesus Christ, Sal," gasped Talia. "What the fuck? I mean—what the fuck?"

Joe Bob swung his big M249 up and dropped the bipod legs on the top sandbag. "I can drop that freak right—"

"Hold your goddamn fire," I growled, and the command in my own voice steadied my feet on the ground. "Farris, Talia—hit the line, but nobody fires a shot unless I say so."

They all looked at me.

"Right fucking now," I bellowed.

They jumped. Farris and Talia brought up their M4 carbines. So did I. The kid was ten yards away now, and he didn't look like he wanted to stop.

"How's he even walking with all that?" asked Talia in a small voice.

I yelled at the civvie. "Hey! Sir? Sir...? I need you to stop right there."

His head jerked up a little more. He had no nose at all. And both eyes were bloodshot and wild. He kept walking, though.

"Sir! Stop. Do not approach the barricade."

He didn't stop.

Then everyone was yelling at him. Ordering him to stop. Telling him to stand down, or lie down, or kneel. Confusing, loud, conflicting. We yelled at the top of our voices as the kid walked right at us.

"I can take him," said Joe Bob in a trembling voice. Was it fear, or was he getting ready to bust a nut at the thought of squeezing that trigger?

The civvie was right there. Right in our faces.

He hit the chest-high stack of sandbags and made a grab for me with his bloody fingers. I jumped back.

There was a sudden, three-shot rat-a-tat-tat.

The civvie flew back from the sandbags, and the world seemed to freeze as the echoes of those three shots bounced off the bridge, and the trees on either side of the river, and the flowing water beneath us. Three drum-hits of sound.

I stared at the shooter.

Not Joe Bob. He was as dumbfounded as me.

Talia's face was white with shock at what she had just done.

"Oh...god..." she said, in a voice that was almost no voice at all. Tiny, lost.

Farris and I were in motion the next second, both of us scrambling over the barricade. Talia stood with her smoking rifle pointed at the sky. Joe Bob gaped at her.

I hit the blacktop and rushed over to where the kid lay sprawled on the ground.

The three-shot burst had caught him in the center of the chest, and the impact had picked him up and dropped him five feet back. His shirt was torn open over a ragged hole.

"Ah...Christ," I said under my breath, and I probably said it forty times as we knelt down.

"We're up the creek on this," said Farris, low enough so Talia couldn't hear.

Behind us, though, she called out, "Is he okay? Please tell me he's okay."

You could have put a beer can in the hole in his chest. Meat and bone were ripped apart; he'd been right up against the barrel when she'd fired.

The kid's eyes were still open.

Wide open.

Almost like they were looking right at...

The dead civvie came up off the ground and grabbed Farris by the hair.

Farris screamed and tried to pull back. I think I just blanked out for a second. I mean...this was impossible. Guy had a fucking hole in his chest and no face and...

Talia and Joe Bob screamed, too.

Then the civvie clamped his teeth on Farris's wrist.

I don't know what happened next. I lost it. We all lost it. One second I was kneeling there, watching Farris hammer at the teenager's face with one fist while blood shot up from between the bastard's teeth. I blinked, and then suddenly the kid was on the ground and the four of us—all of us—were in a circle around him, stomping the shit out of him. Kicking and stamping down and grinding on his bones.

The kid didn't scream.

And he kept twisting and trying to grab at us. With broken fingers and shattered bones in his arms, he kept reaching. With his teeth kicked out, he kept trying to bite. He would not stop.

We would not stop.

None of us could.

And then Farris grabbed his M4 with bloody hands and fired down at the body as the rest of us leapt back. Farris had it on three-round burst mode. His finger jerked over and over on the trigger and he burned through an entire magazine in a couple of seconds. Thirty rounds. They chopped into the kid. They ruined him. They tore his chest and stomach apart. They blew off his left arm. The tore away what was left of his face.

Farris was screaming.

He dropped the magazine and went to swap in a new one, and then I was in his face. I shoved him back.

"Stop it!" I yelled as loud as I could.

Farris staggered and fell against the sandbags, and I was there with him, my palms on his chest, both of us staring holes into each other, chests heaving, ears ringing from the gunfire. His rifle dropped to the blacktop and fell over with a clatter.

The whole world was suddenly quiet. We could hear the run of water in the river, but all of the birds in the trees had shut up.

Joe Bob made a small mewling sound.

I looked at him.

He was looking at the kid.

So I looked at the kid, too.

He was a ragdoll, torn and empty.

The son of a bitch was still moving.

"No," I said.

But the day said: yes.

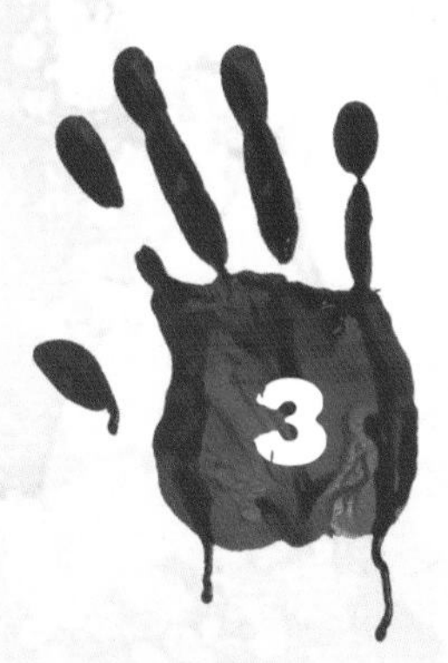

We stood around it.

Not him. It.

What else would you call something like this?

"He...can't still be alive," murmured Talia. "That's impossible."

It was like the fifth or sixth time she'd said that.

No one argued with her.

Except the kid was still moving. He had no lower jaw and half of his neck tendons were shot away, but he kept trying to raise his head. Like he was still trying to bite.

Farris clapped a hand to his mouth and tried not to throw up...but why should he be any different? He spun off and vomited onto the road. Joe Bob and Talia puked in the weeds.

Talia turned away and stood behind Farris, her hand on his back. She bent low to say something to him, but he kept shaking his head.

"What the hell we going to do 'bout this?" asked Joe Bob.

When I didn't answer, the other two looked at me.

"He's right, Sally," said Talia. "We have to do something. We can't leave him like that."

"I don't think a Band-Aid's going to do much frigging good," I said.

"No," she said, "we have to—you know—put him out of his misery."

I gaped at her. "What, you think I'm packing Kryptonite bullets? You shot him, and he didn't die, and Farris...Christ, look at this son of a bitch. What the hell do you think I'd be able to—"

Talia got up and strode over to me and got right in my face.

"Do something," she said coldly.

I wasn't backing down because there was nowhere to go. "Like fucking what?"

Her eyes held mine for a moment and then she turned, unslung her rifle, put the stock to her shoulder, and fired a short burst into the civvie's head.

If I hadn't hurled my lunch a few minutes ago, I'd have lost it now. The kid's head just flew apart.

Blood and gray junk splattered everyone.

Farris started to cry.

The thunder of the burst rolled past us, and the breeze off the river blew away the smoke.

The civvie lay dead.

Really dead.

I looked at Talia. "How—?"

There was no bravado on her face. She was white as a sheet, and half a step from losing her shit. "What else was there to shoot?" she demanded.

I called it in.

We were back on our side of the sandbags. The others hunkered down around me. The kid lay where he was.

Lieutenant Bell said, “You’re sure he stopped moving after taking a headshot?”

I’m not sure what I expected the loot to say, but that wasn’t it. That was a mile down the wrong road from the right kind of answer. I think I’d have felt better if he reamed me out or threatened some kind of punishment. That, at least, would have made sense.

“Yes, sir,” I said. “He, um, did not seem to respond to body shots or other damage.”

I left him a big hole so he could come back at me on this. I wanted him to.

Instead, he said, “We’re hearing this from other posts. Headshots seem to be the only thing that takes these things down.”

“Wait, wait,” I said. “What do you mean ‘these things’? This was just a kid.”

“No,” he said. There was a rustling sound, and I could tell that he was moving, and when he spoke again, his voice was hushed. “Sal, listen to me. The shit is hitting the fan. Not just here, but everywhere.”

“What shit? What the hell’s going on?”

“They...don’t really know. All they’re saying is that it’s spreading like crazy. Western Pennsylvania, Maryland, parts of Virginia and Ohio. It’s all over, and people are acting nuts. We’ve been getting some crazy-ass reports.”

“Come on, Loot,” I said—and I didn’t like the pleading sound in my own voice. “Is this some kind of disease or something?”

“Yes,” he said, then, “Maybe. We don’t know. They don’t know, or if they do, then they’re sure as shit not telling us.”

“But—”

“The thing is, Sally, you got to keep your shit tight. You hear me? You blockade that bridge, and I don’t care who shows up—nobody gets across. I don’t care if it’s a nun with an orphan or a little girl with her puppy, you put them down.”

“Whoa, wait a frigging minute,” I barked, and everyone around me jumped. “What the hell are you saying?”

“You heard me. That kid you put down was infected.”

The others were listening to this, and their faces looked sick and scared. Mine must have, too.

“Okay,” I said, “so maybe he was infected, but I’m not going to open up on everyone who comes down the road. That’s crazy.”

“It’s an order.”

“Bullshit. No one’s going to give an order like that. No disrespect here, Lieutenant, but are you fucking high?”

“That’s the order, now follow it...”

“No way. I don’t believe it. You can put me up on charges, Loot, but I am not going to—”

“Hey!” snapped Bell. “This isn’t a goddamn debate. I gave you an order and—”

“And I don’t believe it. Put the captain

on the line or come here with a signed order from him or someone higher, but I'm not going to death row because you're suddenly losing your shit."

The line went dead.

We sat there and stared at each other.

Ferris rubbed his fingers over the bandage Talia had used to dress his bite. His eyes were jumpy.

"What's going on?" he asked. It sounded like a simple question, but we all knew that it wasn't. That question was a tangle of all sorts of barbed wire and broken junk.

I got up and walked over to the wall of sandbags.

We'd stacked them two deep and chest high, but suddenly it felt as weak as a little picket fence. We still had a whole stack of empty bags we hadn't filled yet. We didn't think we'd need to, and they were heavy as shit. I nudged them with the toe of my boot.

I didn't even have to ask. Suddenly we were all filling the bags and building the wall higher and deeper. In the end, we used every single bag.

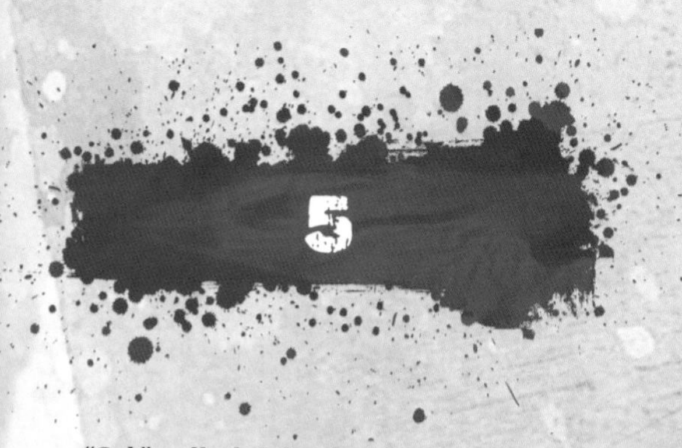

"Sal," called Talia, holding up the walkie-talkie, "the Loot's calling."

I took it from her, but it wasn't Lieutenant Bell, and it wasn't the captain, either.

"Corporal Tucci?" said a gruff voice that I didn't recognize.

"Yes, sir, this is Tucci."

"This is Major Bradley."

Farris mouthed, Oh shit.

"Sir!" I said, and actually straightened like I was snapping to attention.

"Lieutenant Bell expressed your concerns over the orders he gave you."

Here it comes, I thought. I'm dead or I'm in Leavenworth.

"Sir, I—"

"I understand your concerns, Corporal," he said. "Those concerns are natural; they show compassion and an honorable adherence to the spirit of who we are as soldiers of this great nation."

Talia rolled her eyes and mimed shoveling shit, but the Major's opening salvo was scaring me. It felt like a series of jabs before an overhand right.

"But we are currently faced with extraordinary circumstances that are unique in my military experience," continued Major Bradley. "We are confronted by a situation in which our fellow citizens are the enemy."

"Sir, I don't—"

He cut me off. "Let me finish, Corporal. You need to hear this."

"Yes, sir. Sorry, sir."

He cleared his throat. "We are facing a biological threat of an unknown nature. It is very likely a terrorist weapon of some kind, but, quite frankly, we don't know. What we do know is that the infected are a serious threat. They are violent, they are mentally deranged, and they will attack anyone with whom they come into contact, regardless of age, sex, or any other consideration. We have reports of small children attacking grown men.

Anyone who is infected becomes violent. Old people, pregnant women…it, um… doesn't seem to matter." Bradley faltered for a moment, and I wondered if the first part of what he'd said was repeated from orders he got, and if now he was on his own. We all waited.

And waited.

Finally, I said, "Sir?"

But there was no answer.

I checked the walkie-talkie. It was functioning, but Major Bradley had stopped transmitting.

"What the hell?" I said.

"Maybe there's interference," suggested Joe Bob.

I looked around. "Who's got a cell?"

We all had cell phones.

We all called.

I called my brother Vinnie in Newark.

"Sal—Christ on a stick, have you seen the news?" he growled. "Everyone's going ape-shit."

"SAL!"

I spun around and saw Talia pointing past the sandbags.

"They're coming!"

They.

God. They.

The road was thick with them. Maybe forty. Maybe fifty.

All kinds of them.

Guys in suits. Women in skirts and blouses. Kids. A diner waitress in a pink uniform. A man dressed in surgical scrubs. People.

Just people.

Them.

They didn't rush us.

They walked down the road toward the bridge. I think that was one of the worst parts of it. I might have been able to deal with a bunch of psychos running at me. That would have felt like an attack. You see a mob running batshit at you and you switch your M4s to rock'n'roll and hope that all of them are right with Jesus.

But they walked.

Walked.

Badly. Some of them limped. I saw one guy walking on an ankle that you could see was broken from fifty yards out. It was buckled over to the side, but he didn't give a shit. There was no wince, no flicker of emotion on his face.

The whole bunch of them were like that. None of them looked right. They were bloody. They were ragged.

They were mauled.

"God almighty," whispered Farris.

Talia began saying a Hail Mary.

I heard Joe Bob saying, "Fuck yeah, fuck yeah, fuck yeah." But something in his tone didn't sell it for me. His face was greasy with sweat and his eyes were jumpier than a speed freak's.

The crowd kept coming to us. I hung up on Vinnie.

"They're going to crawl right over these damn sandbags," complained Farris. The bandage around his wrist was soaked through with blood. "What do we do?"

He already knew.

When they were fifteen yards away, we opened up.

We burned through at least a mag each before we remembered about shooting them in the head.

Talia screamed it first, and then we were all screaming it. "The head! Shoot for the head!"

"Switch to semi-auto," I hollered. "Check your targets, conserve your ammo."

We stood in a line, our barrels flashing and smoking, spitting fire at the people as they crowded close.

They went down.

Only if we took them in the head. Only then.

At that range, though, we couldn't miss. They walked right up to the barrels. They looked at us as we shot them.

"Jesus, Sal," said Talia as we swapped our mags, "Their eyes. Did you see their eyes?"

I didn't say anything. I didn't have to. When someone is walking up to you and not even ducking away from the shot, you see everything.

We burned through three-quarters of our ammunition.

The air stank of smoke and blood.

Farris was the last one to stop shooting. He was laughing as he clicked on empty, but when he looked back at the rest of us, we could see that there were tears pouring down his cheeks.

The smoke clung to the moment, and for a while, that's all I could see. My mouth was a thick paste of cordite and dry spit. When the breeze came up off the river, we stared into the reality of what we had just done.

"They were all sick, right?" asked Talia. "I mean…they were all infected, right? All of them?"

"Yeah," I said, but what the hell did I know?

We stood there for a long time. None of us knew what the hell to do.

Later, when I tried to call the Major again, I got nothing.

The same thing with the cells. I couldn't even get a signal.

None of us could.

"Come on," I said after a while, "check your ammo."

We did. We had two magazines each, except for Farris, who had one.

Two mags each.

It didn't feel like it was going to be enough.

Talia grabbed my sleeve. "What the hell do we do?"

They all looked at me. Like I knew what the fuck was what.

"We hold this fucking bridge," I said.

No more of them came down the road.

Not then.

Not all afternoon.

Couple of times we heard—or thought we heard—gunfire from way upriver. Never lasted long.

The sun started to fall behind the trees, and it smeared red light over everything. Looked like the world was on fire. I saw Talia staring at the sky for almost fifteen minutes.

"What?" I asked.

"Planes," she said.

I looked up. Way high in the sky there were some contrails, but it was getting too dark to see what they were. Something flying in formation, though.

Joe Bob was on watch, and he was talking to himself. Some Bible stuff. I didn't want to hear what it was.

Instead, I went to the Jersey side of the bridge and looked up and down the road. Talia and Farris came with me, but there was nothing to see.

"Maybe they made a public service announcement," said Talia. "Like the Emergency Broadcast Network thing. Maybe they told everyone to stay home, stay off the roads."

"Sure," I said, in pretty much the same way you'd say "bullshit."

We watched the empty road as the sky grew darker.

"We could just leave," said Farris. "Head up the road. There's that Quiznos. Maybe we can find a ride."

"We can't leave the bridge," I said.

"Fuck the bridge."

I got up in his face. "Really? You want to let them just stroll across the bridge? Is that your plan? Is that what you think will get the job done?"

"What job? We're all alone out here. Might as well be on the far side of the goddamn moon."

"They'll come back for us," I said. "You watch; in the morning there'll be a truck with supplies, maybe some hot coffee."

"Sure," he said, in exactly the same way I had a minute ago.

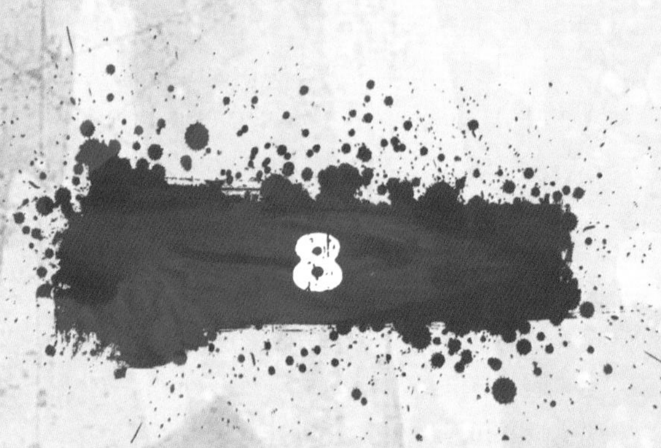

That night, there were a million stars and a bright, three-quarter moon. Plenty of light to see the road. Only one of them came down the road. Talia was on watch, and she took it out with a single shot to the head. She let the thing—it used to be a mailman—walk right up to the sandbags. It opened its mouth, even though it was too far away to bite, and Talia shot it in the eye.

Then she sat down and cried like a little girl for ten whole minutes. I stood her watch and let her cry. I wished I could do that. For me, it was all stuck inside, and it was killing me that I couldn't let it go.

Farris got sick in the night.

I heard him throwing up, and I came over and shined my flashlight on him. His face was slick with sweat. Joe Bob went back to the wall and Talia knelt next to me. She knew more first aid than I did, and she took Farris's vitals as best she could.

"Wow, he's burning up," she said, looking at his fever-bright eyes and sweaty face, but then she put her palm on his forehead and frowned. "That's weird. He's cold."

"Shock?" I asked, but she didn't answer. Then she examined the bite and I heard her gasp. When I shined my light on Farris's arm, I had to bite my lip. The wound on Farris's wrist was bad enough, but there were weird black lines running all the way up his arm. It was like someone had used a Sharpie to outline every vein and capillary.

"It's infection," said Talia, but I knew that it was worse than that.

"God," gasped Farris, "it's blood poisoning."

I said nothing, because I thought it was worse than that, too. Even in the harsh glare of the flashlight, his color looked weird.

Talia met my eyes over the beam of the light. She didn't say anything, but we had a whole conversation with that one look.

I patted Farris on the shoulder. "You get some sleep, man. In the morning we'll get a medic down here to give you a shot, set you right."

Fear was jumping up in his eyes. "You sure? They can give me something for this?"

"Yeah. Antibiotics and shit."

Talia fished in her first-aid kit. There was a morphine syrette. She showed it to me and I nodded.

"Sweet dreams, honey," she said, as she jabbed Farris with the little needle. His eyes held hers for a moment, and then he was out.

We made sure he was comfortable, and then we got up and began walking up and down the length of the bridge. Talia kept looking up at the moon.

"Pretty night," I said.

She made a face.

"Should be a pretty night," I amended.

We stopped for a moment and looked down at the rushing water. It was running fast and high after that big storm a couple of days ago, and each little wave-tip gleamed with silver moonlight. Maybe fifteen, twenty minutes passed while we stood there, our shoulders a few inches apart, hands on the cold metal rail, watching the river do what rivers do.

"Sally?" she asked softly.

"Yeah?"

"This is all happening, right?"

I glanced at her. "What do you mean?"

She used her fingers to lightly trace circles on the inside of her forearm. "You know I used to ride the spike, right? I mean, that's not news."

"I figured."

"I've been getting high most of my life. Since…like seventh grade. Used to swipe pills from my mom's purse. She did a lot of speed, so that's what I started on. Rode a lot of fast waves, y'know?"

"Yeah." I was never much of a hophead, but I lived in Newark and I'd seen a lot of my friends go down in flames.

"Until I got clean the last time, I was probably high more than I was on the ground."

I said nothing.

"So," she continued, "I seen a lot of weird shit. While I was jonesing for a hit, while I was high, on the way down. You lose touch, y'know?"

"Yeah."

"People talk about pink elephants and polka-dotted lobsters and shit, but that's not what comes out of the woodwork." She shivered and gripped the rail with more force. Like it was holding her there. "And not a day goes by—not a fucking day—when I don't want a fix. Even now, twenty-three months clean, I can feel it. It's like worms crawling under my skin. That morphine? You think I haven't dreamed about that every night?"

I nodded. "My Uncle Tony's been in and out of twelve steps for booze. I've seen how he looks at Thanksgiving when the rest of us are drinking beers and watching the ball game. Like he'd take a knife to any one of us for a cold bottle of Coors."

"Right. Did your uncle ever talk to you about having a dry drunk? About feeling stoned and even seeing the spiders come crawling out of the sofa when he hasn't even had a drop?"

"Couple times."

"I get that," she said. "I get that a lot."

I waited.

"That's why I need you to tell me that this is all really happening; or am I lost inside my own head?"

I turned to her and touched her arm. "I wish to Christ and the baby Jesus that I could say that you're just tripping. Having a dry drunk, or whatever you'd call it. A flashback—whatever. But…I ain't a drunk and I never shot up, and here I am, right with you. Right here in the middle of this shit."

Talia closed her eyes and leaned her forehead on the backs of the hands that clung so desperately to the rail. "Ah…fuck," she said quietly.

I felt like a total asshole for telling her the truth.

Then Talia stiffened, and I saw that she was looking past her hands. "What's that?"

"What?"

She pointed over the rail. "In the water. Is that a log, or…?"

Something bobbed up and down as the current swept it toward the bridge. It looked black in the moonlight, but as it came closer we could see that part of it was white.

The face.

White.

We stared at it…and it stared back up at us.

Its mouth was open, working, like it was trying to bite us even as the river pulled it under the bridge and then out the other side. We hurried to the other side and stared over, watching the thing reach toward us, its white fingers clawing the air.

Then it was gone. A shape, then a dot, then nothing.

Neither of us could say a word.

Until the next one floated by. And the next.

"God, no…" whispered Talia.

We went back to the other side of the bridge.

"There's another," I said. "No…two…no…"

I stopped counting.

Counting didn't matter.

Who cares how many of them floated down? Two, three hundred? A thousand?

After the first one, really, who cared how many?

Talia and I stood there all night, watching. There were ordinary civilians and people in all kinds of uniforms. Cops, firemen, paramedics. Soldiers. I wished to God that I had a needle of heroin for her. And for me.

We didn't tell the others.

I'm not sure what time the bodies stopped floating past. The morning was humid, and there was a thick mist. It covered the river, and maybe there were still bodies down there, or maybe the fog hid them.

We stood there as the fog curled gray fingers around the bridge and pulled itself up to cover everything. The wall of sandbags, Joe Bob, the sleeping figure of Farris, our gear. All of it.

Talia and I never moved from the rail, even when it got hard to see each other.

"They'll come for us, right?" she asked. "The Lieutenant? The supply truck? They'll come to get us, right?"

"Absolutely," I said. She was a ghost beside me.

"You're sure?"

"They'll come."

And they did.

It wasn't long, either, but the sun was already up and the fog was starting to thin out. Talia saw them first and she stiffened.

"Sally..."

I turned to look.

At first it was only a shape. A single figure, and my heart sank. It came down the road from the direction our truck had come, walking wearily toward us from the Jersey side. In the fog it was shapeless, shambling.

Talia whimpered, just a sound of denial that didn't have actual words.

"Fuck me," I whispered, but before I could even bring my gun up, the fog swirled, and I could see the mishmash stripes of camouflage, the curve of a helmet, the sharp angles of a rifle on its sling.

Talia grabbed my arm. "Sally, look!"

There was movement behind the soldier, and, one by one, shapes emerged. More camos, more tin pots.

More soldiers.

They came walking down the road. Five of them. Then more.

"It's the whole platoon," Talia said, and laughter bubbled in her voice.

But it was more than that. As the mist thinned, I could see a lot of soldiers. A hundred at least. More.

"Damn," I said, "they look bone-ass tired. They must have been fighting all night."

"Is it over?" she asked. "Have we beaten this goddamn thing?"

I smiled. "I think so."

I waved, but no one waved back. Some of them could barely walk. I could understand; I felt like I could drop where I stood. We'd been up all night watching the river.

"Talia, go wake up Farris and tell Joe

Bob to look sharp."

She grinned and spun away and vanished into the veil of fog that still covered the bridge.

I took a second to straighten my uniform and sling my rifle the right way. I straightened my posture and stepped off the bridge onto the road, looking tough, looking like someone who maybe should get some sergeant's stripes for holding this frigging bridge. Army strong, booyah.

I saw Lieutenant Bell, and he was as wrung out as the rest of them. He lumbered through the fog, shoulders slumped, and behind him were gray soldiers. Even from this distance I could tell that no one was smiling. And for a moment, I wondered if maybe this was a retreat rather than a surge. Shit. Had they gotten their asses kicked, and these were the survivors? If so…Bell would have his ass handed to him and I wouldn't be going up a pay grade.

"Well, whatever," I said to myself. "Fireteam Delta held the bridge, so fuck it and fuck you and hooray for the red, white, and blue."

A breeze wandered out of the south and blew past me, swirling the mist, blowing it off the bridge and pushing it away from the soldiers. The mass of gray figures changed into khaki and brown and green.

And red.

All of them.

Splashed with…

I turned and screamed at the top of my lungs. "TALIA! Joe Bob, Farris! Lock and load. Hostiles on the road…"

The breeze had blown all the mist off of the bridge.

Talia stood forty feet from the wall of sandbags. Her rifle hung from its sling, the sling in her hand, the stock of the weapon on the blacktop. She stood, her back to me, staring at Joe Bob.

At what was left of Joe Bob.

Farris must have heard something. Maybe a sound I made, or Talia's first scream. He froze in the midst of lifting something from Joe Bob's stomach. Some piece of something. I couldn't tell what, didn't care what.

Farris bared his teeth at us.

Then he stuffed the thing into his mouth and chewed.

Where he wasn't covered with blood, Farris's skin was gray-green and veined with black lines.

Behind me I heard the shuffling steps of the soldiers as the first of them left the road and stepped onto the bridge.

Talia turned toward me, and in her eyes, I saw everything that had to be in my own eyes.

Her fingers twitched, and the rifle dropped to the asphalt.

"Please," she said. Her mouth trembled into a smile. "Please."

Please.

I raised my rifle, racked the bolt, and shot her. She was never a pretty girl. Too thin, too worn by life. She had nice eyes, though, and a nice smile. The bullets took that away, and she fell back.

I heard—felt—someone come up behind me.

Something.

Probably Bell.

I turned. I still only had two mags. Less three bullets.

There were hundreds of them.

I fired.